The Leather Jacket

By Lisa Sa

Illustrated by Dimitry Soloviov

Thank you.

The Leather Jacket

2010

1

When fourteen year-old Valeria arrived at the volleyball tournament that warm August evening, she was hungry, and not for food. She looked around the field at the wide selection of teenage boys. They were exactly her taste – tanned, toned, and ready for her to pounce on.

She preyed on them from a distance of course – fourteen year-old Valeria had never been kissed, let alone done anything else.

She arrived at the volleyball tournament just as the sun was beginning to set, and she strolled onto the field wearing a jeans miniskirt and her favourite red top with white graffiti on it. She loved the skirt because it showed off her tanned legs, and she loved the top because it highlighted her slim figure.

Valeria was a fan of grunge bands and boys. That was it. Nothing else in the world mattered. She didn't get along well with her parents as they were strict and never let her out back in the city, whilst her friends were already out there getting drunk at parties. They did however let her roam free when they came to the small town, seeing since there were no more than a thousand residents and it was a pretty damn safe place to be. It was a pity then that, where Valeria was allowed to roam free, was in a place that Valeria detested.

She hated going to the countryside every summer, she hated staying in the small town, and she hated making small talk with people she didn't know.

As she made her way over to the volleyball game, she spotted five 'fitties' along the way, and made a mental note for her diary later. She loved to describe the beautiful boys she saw in her diary; it gave her a sense of satisfaction. She smiled at every cute boy who passed her, and they smiled right back, their eyes checking her out from head to toe. Tall, short, blonde, brunette – they were all gorgeous and all her crush for the next five – ten seconds.

She looked out at the supposed 'volleyball court' and sighed in disappointment. It was a particularly pathetic set up, especially for a tournament between the small town and three adjacent ones. She couldn't believe it was taking place on a field.

Instead of sand there was grass, and instead of a strong net there was a very sad and very tattered half-net that divided the opponents. Yet everyone in the audience was cheering as if it was *the* most serious game of the year.

Small towns, Valeria thought to herself as she shook her head. She studied the two boys currently playing as she circled the supposed court to get to the juice table – they were both gorgeous and everything she had ever wanted. She eyed them both, and they both eyed her.

She loved to have this effect on boys. At fourteen, she was beginning to feel less like a kid, and more like a girl. A girl that was realising the power she could have on the opposite sex.

"Want some juice?" asked the town chatterbox, Barbara, as she held out a plastic cup. Valeria knew Barbara only by name and the occasional 'hi' when they would pass each other on the street every summer. Yet it felt like they were neighbours all year round.

Valeria's parents visited the small town every year without fail. They were good friends with the town hippie, Pattie, who had gone to school with Valeria's mum in the city and then moved to the countryside. Valeria's parents had fallen in love with the small town so much over the years that when Valeria turned eight, they had bought a house there and turned the occasional visit into a yearly tradition.

Valeria however found the small town terribly boring. Having been born and raised in the big city, she expected big lights and big entertainment, everywhere she went. The small town didn't give her any of that, and so she resented the place. She was young and innocent, and she couldn't wait to get rid of all that. To live, and make mistakes, and do things with boys.

"Yes please," Valeria said to Barbara, who poured her a cup. She took in the loud cheering and banter going on around her, and enjoying watching the sun slowly start to set in the background.

As Valeria began to glaze over the audience for more guys to mentally undress with her eyes, she suddenly felt something hit her abruptly on the thigh. It stung.

"Ow! What the…?" she looked down to find a volleyball bouncing pathetically in the grass beside her. She realised it had been from the game just as she heard footsteps and looked up to find a boy grinding to a halt in front of her.

He kneeled to pick it up, and when he rose, their eyes met for the first time. When they did, Valeria had to bite her lip to stop herself from gasping as she studied the boy.

His eyes were ocean blue, his face tanned, and his body toned. He had freckles on his neck and a couple on his face that Valeria wanted to kiss and lick and–

She told her libido to hush as she gulped. He was wearing faded blue jeans, and a weird t-shirt that had only one sleeve. It was an odd wardrobe choice, especially as Valeria had never seen such an item of clothing before, but she put it down to small town fashion trends.

"I'm so sorry!" he said, and he studied every inch of her face as he spoke. "That was my fault!"

Valeria wanted to say something, she really did, but she was too stunned. Her voice box had gone completely dry in only a matter of seconds, and she instead continued to stare at him, just as he continued to stare at her.

It went on for what seemed like an eternity. From all the boys Valeria had crushed on in the past three weeks in the small town, nothing compared to the boy standing in front of her now.

Sure, he was toned and tanned like most of the other boys on that field, but there was something in his eyes – a charisma, a spark, that had Valeria's attention like no other boy before him. Not even back in the city.

"*Leo!* Come on, let's go!" shouted the boy's competition in a frustrated tone. "Haven't got all day!"

Both Valeria and Leo snapped out of their stare, and she noticed that the entire crowd of spectators were now leering at them.

"Leo, what are you doing?" yelled Barbara, a little too fiercely for just a friendly neighbour.

"I'm going, mum!" the beautiful boy replied, and he gave Valeria a quick smile again before jogging back onto the court with the volleyball.

Did he just say 'mum'?! Valeria thought to herself.

She gulped down her cup of orange juice and realised she was instantly hooked, with a multitude of questions.

Why hadn't she seen him around town before? It was a tiny town. If Barbara was his mother, then he definitely lived in this town.

How could she have missed such a person? Such a face? Such a smile?

She was desperate to know everything about him, instantly, and luckily for her, she had the perfect source right in front of her.

"I had no idea you had children," Valeria told Barbara.

"Oh, I have two kids – a girl, nine, and that one over there is fifteen. He does half scare me to death when he takes out the motorbike though, God almighty..."

At the mention of a motorbike Valeria felt a tingle in her private parts. She was obsessed with them, even if she had never ridden one. She had always wanted to; to feel the breeze in her air, to hold onto a strong, toned chest as they rode through the beautiful mountains together. She knew that she wanted her moments on a motorbike to take place in the countryside; the big city was too crowded for such a pleasure.

"Motorbike?" Valeria croaked.

"Yes dear, he's not old enough for a proper one yet but he steals his cousin's or goes out on his moped. Drives like a maniac – thinks he's James Dean or something."

"Oh really?" This was only getting worse for Valeria. The more she learned about this beautiful stranger, the more she wanted to know him. Or more, shove her tongue down his throat.

Fourteen year-old Valeria sat herself down on the bench with Barbara, as the town chatterbox began to tell her everything there was to know about her son.

As she listened to Barbara natter away as if her son were a famous celebrity and Valeria the news reporter, she conveniently decided there and then, that somehow, and she didn't know how yet, but she was going to make sure that he became a part of her life.

2012

2

When sixteen-year old Valeria arrived outside Pattie's door and knocked, she sighed and tried to force a smile as she heard footsteps on the other side.

Valeria was not exactly glad to be back in the small town. After convincing her parents to instead go to the Bahamas the previous summer, it seemed she couldn't shake their desire to return to the countryside for too long. She was tired of being bossed around and treated like a kid. She was an adult, or nearly, and if she wanted to stay in the big city over the summer, she should have been able to. She was old enough to stay at home by herself.

"Oh my, you're back!" Pattie wailed, as she pulled Valeria into a hug. "Aren't you glad to be back?!"

"Sure Pattie, of course."

When sixteen-year-old Valeria returned to the small town, it had been exactly two years since she had first laid eyes on the mysterious blonde at the volleyball tournament. A lot had changed in that time.

For starters, Valeria no longer looked about ten – she had grown up, changed her hair, her wardrobe, and her taste in music. All for the better, of course. Now not only did she love grunge music but also sub genres of indie rock.

No longer was her hair long and uncared for, but shoulder length, prim and slick. Her love of mini skirts was still very much intact, though they were now less 'skater girl' and more lady like.

After locking eyes with the blonde stranger that fateful night two years earlier, Valeria had been determined to meet him, to know him, to have him in her life. She was however also a firm believer in the guy making the first move, and so instead of simply approaching him and introducing herself, she had spent a hell of a long time planning out plenty of perfect opportunities for him to approach her.

From learning what time he left the house to meet his friends (because of course she found out where he lived – it was a small town after all), to what time he usually took out the moped on weekends, to what parks he went to, she made the effort to be 'around' when he left the house. Always looking gorgeous, and always with a book in hand. She never went anywhere without one. Stalking was, for the most part, rather boring and she needed some entertainment.

The blonde stranger would see her, they would lock eyes, smile, sometimes he would even stare, but he never once attempted to approach her.

This infuriated Valeria. By the end of the summer, Valeria had given up, and once she was back in the city, she focused her attention on other handsome boys. At fourteen, there were plenty around, and plenty willing to give her attention. But none of them seemed to have the same impact on her the way the freckled blonde had.

Being back in the small town an entire two years on, Valeria found herself wondering if she'd see him somewhere. It was, after all, a town where everyone knew each other. But she didn't give it too much thought; he would likely not approach her anyway, and Valeria had no interest in him. Not the way she had when she was fourteen, anyway. She was a grown up now, and she wanted to be back in the city as fast as she could.

She was already insanely bored.

"Cheer up chica, did your parents send you here for breakfast?" Pattie asked, pulling her inside and closing the door.

"Yep, they said they'll be along in a bit."

Pattie was in her late forties, a chiropractor, and an all round hippie of the modern age. i.e. she wore tons of bright clothes and preached about peace every chance she could.

She helped out with any of the town festivities – from making the clothes for school plays, to giving speeches at town events. Valeria found her slightly lame for her small town ways, but she also used to be a corporate lawyer and lived in the city too, so Valeria was convinced that a part of her was still a big city girl.

"Oh, before we eat, you gotta go to the garden for a sec! There's someone that wants to see you!"

Valeria frowned. "Who?" she asked, trying to think who could possibly be awaiting her arrival.

Ferguson, from next door? But I saw him on my way here?

Tommy from the bakery?

Sara from the bakery?!

"Leo!"

As soon as Valeria heard the name 'Leo' uttered from Pattie's mouth, it took every fibre of her being to refrain her jaw from dropping.

She had flashbacks of the volleyball tournament – the mysterious blonde's smile, his sweet 'sorry!' as they had looked at one another.

Valeria began trembling, as she had flashbacks of all the times they had passed each other on the street two years ago, smiled at each other, but never said a word to each other.

She remembered the pain she had felt on her leg when the volleyball had hit her that evening two years ago, the way his eyes had made her heart ache for him, without knowing a thing about him.

Snapping back to reality, Valeria didn't understand what was happening.

Had she met him before and simply blocked it out of her memory?

Why was he here?

And why did he want to see her, when they had never previously spoken before?

"Who?" Valeria managed to say, pretending she didn't know him, because she had never told Pattie about her obsession with him. She had never told anyone.

"Oh you know Leo, don't you? He lives up the road? His mother is Barbara? You know him, right? He says he knows you and when I told him you were coming back today he wanted to see you!"

Valeria gulped, as butterflies hit her stomach. She could hardly believe this was really happening, and her head began spinning as she tried to understand how on Earth he knew her.

Wait a minute, is Leo friends with Pattie?

"You two know each other?" Valeria asked her, curiously.

"This is a small town, lovey. I knew of him for many years of course, heard of the town antics he'd get up to - he's a bit troublesome, and a lot of people, well, they don't like him. He gets up to mischief and he speaks his mind at town meetings. To be honest, I didn't really want much to do with him.

But then I officially met him at Rosie's one afternoon – and oh, Valeria, he's so lovely. I can see why you are friends with him. He's been helping me with persuading the local council to give me a parking space. He's good with that stuff."

As Valeria tried to take in all this new information about the mysterious blonde - the trouble he seemed to cause the town and the fact that he was now Pattie's friend, she was suddenly pushed through the house to the back door.

"Go, go, before they leave! Go show off those legs!" Pattie swatted her butt and gently shoved her out the garden door.

Valeria found herself curiously and nervously obeying Pattie's request, walking down the garden path towards the strangers, who all had their backs to her as they chatted away, beer bottles in hands, looking out at the magnificent view of the mountains.

There were three of them - two teenage boys, and Pattie's thirty-something year-old brother, Max.

She heard Pattie hiss "with more swag, girl!" from the kitchen window, and Valeria transformed her walk from nervous and shy, to sexy, confident queen. She walked as if she owned the garden, hell – she owned the town!

And with every step Valeria took, she realised just how much she wanted to see the mysterious blonde. To see what he looked like now – at seventeen. To encounter the infectious smile that two years ago had turned her into a borderline insane person/stalker.

She wanted to find out how he knew her, to officially meet him, to be able to talk to him.

To understand why he was here waiting for her, and how he ended up here.

She was suddenly fourteen again, and ready to get all the answers she needed to kick-start her summer in the small town.

I'm ready for this, Valeria told herself.

I'm so ready for this...

3

As Valeria walked with 'swagger' towards the strangers in Pattie's garden, all three of them continued chatting with their backs to her.

She walked with confidence, and sexiness, and determination towards him, the very blonde that had taken her breath away at age fourteen.

She took a deep breath in, knowing that at any second, they would all turn around and she would officially meet him...

She couldn't wait to see him, to talk to him, to actually become a part of each other's lives and learn about one another. To actually have a conversation with him.

Okay, maybe she had lied to herself a bit. She still thought about him, even after two years. She had come back to the small town with the buried desire to see him.

A lot had happened in two years, and yet her fascination with the blonde stranger had remained.

This had to mean something, right?

When they all turned around and Valeria locked eyes with the blonde for the first time in two years however, she had to resist gasping.

The boy in front of her didn't seem anything like the same person she had seen at the volleyball tournament two years earlier.

His blue eyes were no longer sweet and innocent, curious to explore the world. They were instead two blocks of ice; they held no emotion, and they gave nothing away. His once beautiful blonde hair was now cut so short it was as if they had been punished for existing, and his jaw seemed meaner, tougher, and representing a person you did not want to mess with.

He wore a thick, black leather jacket even though it was the start of summer, and semi-tight black jeans. He looked leaner, bigger and, well...

Like a Bad Boy.

You know, one of those loners who hate the world and every person in it. They wear black and scour the town for trouble – drugs, drag races – you name it, this guy probably did it.

He looked like someone who went looking for trouble, and often found it. He looked like someone that got a kick out of the feel of danger. Because this stranger in front of Valeria wasn't afraid of anything. She felt it instantly.

The innocent, blonde fifteen-year-old kid Valeria had encountered at age fourteen had evaporated into thin air. And one thing was sure – the stranger standing in front of her now wouldn't be caught dead hanging around a volleyball tournament, let alone participating in one. In fact, he'd probably be the one beating up those who did.

How things could change so dramatically in just two years.

The Bad Boy was still good-looking to Valeria, but in a different way. He was no longer a sweet and innocent type of cute that had caught Valeria's attention two years earlier. It was now a cold and an intimidating attraction, with eyes that made you afraid to look at him for too long.

This didn't appeal to Valeria. In fact, she only felt discomfort and disappointment in his presence. And to think she had wasted so many of her nights thinking about him, fantasising about him.

All for nothing.

All for a person who no longer even existed.

What on Earth happened in these two years?!

"Leo, here's Valeria!" exclaimed Max, Pattie's little brother. He always shouted everything he said, as if incapable of talking at a normal decibel.

The Bad Boy dipped his lit cigarette between his lips, and stuck out his hand. "Great to see you again, Valeria."

Liar. Liar. Liar.

We have never officially met, ever.

I used to look at you from a distance, and you at me, but you never approached me.

Not once!

Though Valeria was feeling a myriad of emotions, most of them negative, as soon as their hands touched, she felt an electricity hit her like a ton of bricks.

She gulped, trying to pretend it wasn't happening, but she saw in his eyes that he was experiencing the same thing, and it was funny to see a Bad Boy squirm ever so slightly.

Both of them hadn't expected the electricity currently soaring between them, and yet there it was. As alive and as present as anything else in the universe. As they looked at one another, they both looked just as confused and just as intrigued by the current chemistry they felt.

"And that's Tom," Max said. Valeria and Tom exchanged disinterested nods at one another, as the Bad Boy kept his gaze fixed on Valeria. His eyes were filled with interest and intrigue. As if he had been waiting all day for this moment, which was crazy, because Bad Boys never looked forward to things, ever.

"So how's it going? How was your trip?" Max asked, as he diced some tomatoes on a wooden chop board.

"Was good. A little boring, but that's to be expected. How's it going here?" Valeria asked.

He shrugged. "Same old. Small towns never change." He turned to the Bad Boy. "Anything happening tonight? It'll be Saturday night..."

Valeria now had permission to look back at the Bad Boy. She studied him in more detail, seeing that absolutely everything about him now was rough and rugged, from his facial hair, to his skin.

You are definitely not the boy I saw two summers ago.

She remembered his pure, untouched skin at fifteen. How his freckles had shone in the sunlight, and how his smile could light up the entire town.

Now it looks as though you'd have to pay him a lot of money to get him to smile.

The Bad Boy shrugged coolly, as he inhaled smoke. We all waited for him to breathe out, and he did so slowly, as if he liked holding the attention of an audience.

"There's always things on," he began, and as he did so, Valeria realised that she had no interest in what he had to say. There was no intrigue here, nor fascination. Not anymore. He had simply turned into a Bad Boy, and Valeria didn't like Bad Boys. They were just assholes hiding behind a tough guy persona.

"...there's a couple of concerts going on tonight, some shows," he continued, turning to Valeria suddenly. "You wanna go to one? They're not going to be as fancy as the ones in the city, but they're good to see, kill some time..."

Wait, what?

Me?

Did he just ask me out?!

As Valeria stared at the Bad Boy, she knew that two years earlier she would have jumped at the chance to go out with him, to talk to him, to spend one-on-one time with him. She imagined fourteen-year-old her appearing next to them, jumping up and down in joy.

However, things were different now, and the person in front of her was different too. They had missed their window, and Valeria was perfectly fine with this. In all sincerity, the thought of going out with the person in front of her made Valeria want to cringe and run away. He was not her type at all. Not anymore.

"Uh, I'm afraid I'm busy tonight. And I have to go back inside now…" she managed to say.

The Bad Boy tried hard to hide his disappointment and gave her a clipped nod. Valeria realised as she studied him that he probably didn't get rejected very often, that the girls in the small town and the adjacent towns probably all loved Bad Boys.

But not Valeria.

"See you around," she said to them all.

As she walked back into the house, Valeria let out a huge sigh of relief, finding she had an urgent need to wash her hands instantly.

I don't ever want to see that chump again! She said to herself, shaking her head in disappointment as she ran her hands under the tap.

4

If dying of boredom was possible I would surely be dead, Valeria thought to herself.

She sat at the dinner table at Pattie's house, playing cards with Pattie and Max. This would be fine on a normal day, sure, but it was Saturday night and sixteen-year-old Valeria desperately wanted to be out there with all the other kids her age.

Okay, not entirely accurate – she wanted to be out there perving on guys her age (and up to six years older), making new friends, and drinking.

Valeria had drunk very few times in her life up until then, and never with her friends. Yes, that's right, her whimsical experiences with alcohol so far in life revolved around sips of red wine on Christmas Day and sips of Champagne on New Year's Eve.

If that wasn't exciting enough, Valeria wasn't doing much better on the romantic front either, having never been out on a date with a boy, kissed one, or even flirted with one. She was virtuous on a myriad of levels.

Yet she was eager to learn, to jump in, to change all of this. After all, she was more than ready.

As she yawned, Valeria thought back to how she had seen the mysterious blonde for the first time in two whole years earlier that day. Except he was no longer the mysterious blonde from the volleyball tournament, he was now the town Bad Boy.

The town criminal.

The town loser.

She had a flashback of the way he had looked at her two years ago, and compared it to the way he had looked at her in Pattie's garden.

Those eyes, so cold.

"Valeria, you okay?" Pattie asked, as she tried to catch a glimpse at Max's cards. They both sat opposite her, giddy with joy over their Saturday night plans. Valeria however had never felt more like a loner.

"Huh? Yes, I'm fine."

"Want more out of your Saturday night, eh?"

It was as if Pattie could see right through Valeria. Though, everyone at that table knew the only alternative was for Valeria to go home and spend Saturday night with her parents.

"You should be out on the town, girl. What are you doing with us oldies?"

"I'm fine, this is fine," Valeria replied, lying through her teeth.

Where else could she go? She didn't have any friends in this town. She tried to think what she had done when she had last visited – explored the adjacent towns during the day, and hung out in her room in the evenings.

Well, she had been fourteen then. Only now were things different, only now was she sixteen. Except she didn't know anyone, and she couldn't get anywhere without a car.

"You should call Leo," Pattie suddenly told her, and Valeria instantly had goose bumps on the back of her neck at the mention of his name. She wasn't used to people saying his name.

Not for two years.

Did she want to hang out with the Town Loser? Not so much. Seventeen-year-old guys trying to act hard and tough were not her thing and she didn't want to spend the entire evening watching that unfold.

However, she also didn't want to stay home on Saturday night and play cards. And well, she liked the idea of riding a motorbike for the first time. She had always loved motorbikes and found them fascinating. She had the chance to ride one now, could she really decline and spend the evening indoors playing cards with two people twenty years her senior?

It looked as though Valeria's desire to both explore nightlife in the countryside and ride a motorbike were bigger than her desire to not hang out with a Bad Boy. She glanced at Pattie, but before she could say something, Max intervened.

"Hey, he left you something," he told her, pulling out a piece of paper from his pocket. Valeria watched him unfold it and hand it to her.

FOR VALERIA

Here's my number

Call me if you change your mind

Valeria couldn't believe it. After she had directly rejected him, he had still left her his number. As if he knew this would happen, as if he knew she would later be so desperate to escape Pattie's, to have an actual Saturday night out in this place, and he was kindly offering his services.

Well, he was thoughtful enough to leave his number.

Shut up, Valeria. He's a stranger, remember?

You two didn't actually meet until a few hours ago!

Yeah but, isn't it time to live a bit, or do you want to remain sheltered your entire life?

"Okay," Valeria said, as she got out her phone and dialled the number. Pattie squealed in excitement, her eyes lighting up in joy at her decision.

Valeria was fine as she dialled, and she was fine as it rang, but as soon as there was a voice on the other side of the line, she immediately panicked.

"You talk!" she demanded to Pattie, almost throwing the phone at her in fright.

"What? Uh, okay...uhm..." Pattie pressed the phone to her ear, calmly. "Leo? Hey, it's Pattie!

No, this is Valeria's phone. She actually changed her mind and would love to go out tonight." Pause. "Excellent. Yes, just come to the house. How long will you be?" Pause. "Fab, yes she'll be ready. Okay Leo, see you then."

Pattie hung up and turned to Valeria with a cheeky grin. "He'll be here to pick you up in twenty minutes, he was just getting ready to leave – we caught him just in time."

Valeria smiled, defying all the embarrassment currently consuming her from having had Pattie organise her date for her. As she did so however, she suddenly felt instantly nauseous.

Wait, what the hell have I just signed up to?

5

Valeria was still sat at the table at Pattie's when the Bad Boy arrived, and she was twitching with nerves. She couldn't believe she had agreed to go on a date with him, and she couldn't understand if she was about to make a horrible decision by doing so.

Yet there was a strange feeling in her stomach, as if she had just opened Pandora's box. She was somehow sure that her choice in that moment would have consequences for years to come. Whether that they were going to be good or bad consequences couldn't yet be determined however.

The doorbell rang and Max ordered the person to come in.

"Hey!" Pattie bellowed moments later, as she popped a couple of salty nuts into her mouth. They all watched the Bad Boy appear shyly at the door of the kitchen. Yes, shyly. The town rebel, or as Valeria was seeing him in that moment – the town idiot, was suddenly shy. She had flashbacks of his smile back at fifteen, glistening in the sun.

He was a different person back then, Valeria.

"Good evening," he managed to say, slightly awkwardly. His eyes glazed over at Valeria, and she only gulped.

"Leo! Come in! Have something to drink!" Pattie told him, waving her hand at him dramatically.

"Uh, thanks Pattie, but I kind of have to go soon..."

As Valeria studied him, she realised that this was his act – the act he put on around adults. He was the shy, responsible teenager. She saw through it in a nanosecond, and realised she was curious to learn the various sides to him.

Maybe this won't be such a bad night after all.

Valeria timidly rose, and did so in such a bundle of nerves that she nearly fell backwards. "Shall we?" she managed to say, trying to sound confident but failing miserably. Valeria didn't understand why she was so nervous when she didn't have any interest in the boy standing in front of her.

"Sure, let's go." He moved to the side to let her pass first, and when Valeria opened the front door she inwardly gasped.

The black Audi in the driveway with the engine on was shiny and slick, but deep down Valeria was disappointed. It wasn't a motorbike.

She hadn't thought for a second that perhaps he would pick her up in a car! That was too normal for the Bad Boy, and she found herself secretly sad that on her first ever date she wasn't going to be whisked away on a sexy motorbike.

That was not the only thing that had Valeria shocked, however. The fact that there was also a twelve-year-old girl sitting in the passenger seat of the Bad Boy's car had Valeria glaring in curiosity.

"I gotta drop off my little sis to a party, that okay?"

That was more than okay for Valeria. She smiled ever so slightly, relieved that someone else was going to be in the car with them for what she knew was going to be one hell of an awkward car journey.

"Sure."

"Stay safe!" Pattie told Valeria, her hands slumped in her jeans. "Don't drink (too much!) and uhm, don't do drugs!"

"Sure. Promise."

The Bad Boy glanced at Valeria and smiled, as they both opened their car doors at the same time. Once they had both slammed them shut, the awkward silence hit them the way Valeria knew it would.

What is it about car journeys that only add any more awkwardness to a situation and remind two people who barely know each other that they are in fact nothing but strangers?

The Bad Boy glanced at his little sister. "Em, this is Valeria."

Emily chose to ignore her big brother, as she continued to do her lipstick in the mirror. Valeria of course already knew that Leo had a little sister called Emily from her stalker skills two years ago.

The journey, as predicted by Valeria, began in painful silence. She decided to distract herself from it by putting on her seat belt. This would have worked fine had she been able to locate it in the darkness of the Bad Boy's car.

She pulled out her phone torch and searched high and low for it, between all the crap that the Bad Boy seemed to keep in his car – boxes and alcohol and empty cigarette boxes.

This is the longest time anyone has ever taken to find their seatbelt.

"Valeria, do you drive?" the Bad Boy asked. She quickly put off her phone torch, and turned to face him in the car mirror. He was looking at her with the same curious eyes he had had outside in the garden earlier in the day.

She saw that his 'shy, responsible adult' persona was still around however, and she wondered how long he would keep this up for.

"No, though I could technically start learning now..."

"Do it! It's so important!" he told her, and again the car was met with silence. Valeria gave it a good ten seconds before switching her phone torch back on and going back to searching for her seat belt.

"You know, I used to see you round town," he suddenly said. This time Valeria didn't even remember to switch off her phone torch, she simply glanced back at him in the mirror.

"What?" she said.

He paused a moment, as if searching for the right words. "This was about two years ago. You would walk around town with a book in hand – sit in the park, or in the orchards.

I wanted to approach you back then, I did, but..." the Bad Boy shrugged. "You looked so into your books. I didn't want to disturb."

Valeria was stunned. All this time, she hadn't thought he had noticed her. In fact, she had thought he had seen right through her, each time they had glanced at one another around town.

He didn't seem to want to approach her, or talk to her, or know who she was. Not the way she had wanted to know him. And my God, how much she had wanted to know him.

Ever since that volleyball tournament two years ago.

They smiled at each other in the mirror, and Valeria realised this was the first time in two years that she had seen him smile. And despite having no interest in him whatsoever, she suddenly felt goose bumps on the back of her neck again.

All at once he cleared his throat, and settled his eyes back on the road. Valeria went back to trying to find her seatbelt, pretending as if what the Bad Boy had just told her had not completely and utterly dumbfounded her.

It was a good ten minutes later that the Bad Boy's little sister slammed the passenger door shut, and the car felt a lot smaller.

Valeria was excited to be alone with the Bad Boy. She was excited to spend the evening with him, and to actually have a date with him. Because two years ago, he had noticed her.

Two years ago, he had seen her.

So what if he's now a little colder, a little tougher, and he thinks he's some sort of James Dean wannabee?

We all go through phases, I should get to know him first before I judge him.

The Bad Boy shuffled about in his seat, his leather jacket squeaking with every move of his arms. He suddenly turned around to look at her. "Wanna move to the front?"

I thought you'd never ask!

To avoid further embarrassment on Valeria's end, she decided that instead of climbing across to the front that she would jump out of the car and back in at the front. As soon as she sat down next to him, it felt as if their bodies were always supposed to be this close.

There was a chemistry sizzling between them, and it was intense. It was exactly the sort of lightning feeling she had felt when they had shaken hands earlier in the day in Pattie's garden.

They *vroomed* off into the black of night, and she noticed that the chemistry between them continued to build with every passing second.

It was a sort of chemistry that she had never felt before in her life, but then again, it wasn't like she had much experience to compare it to.

The Bad Boy drove fast, like really fast. It was the countryside, every road was built on a mountain, and he swerved violently at every turn.

It made Valeria anxious and nauseous at the same time, but she didn't say anything. She didn't want to look weak or like a kid that had never been in a car that was clearly driving over the limit. She instead chose to remain mute, grasping the door handle casually as he swerved round corners.

No matter how nauseous or scared she felt, Valeria chose to remain mute. She would *not* show him her fear.

"So where are we going?" she eventually asked.

It was extremely nerve-wracking for Valeria to be sitting so close to him, but she tried to hide it as hard as she could. She had spent two years wondering how he was doing, if they would ever meet, and here they were. About to share a Saturday night together, their first date, and somehow, she felt like she *knew* that this wouldn't be the last Saturday night they would ever share together.

The Bad Boy looked at her as he drove. When he looked at her, he turned his whole head, as if to give her his full attention, and Valeria noticed that his 'shy, responsible' persona was gone now. He was relaxed, and curious, and himself.

"Oh, we're gonna go to a bar first – Red Flags, ever been?"

Valeria shook her head.

"Well, Red Flags is a popular bar round here, it's the go-to place for before you go out."

"Wait, after that there's more?" Valeria glanced at her watch. "It's 10pm already! And we're still going to the pre-drinks of the night?!"

To Valeria this was a notion she found hard to digest – that people could only be starting their Saturday night after 10pm. Back in the city, Saturday night started at 8pm, and ended at 1am. At least hers did, anyway.

The Bad Boy chortled. "Wow, I can see you really live it up in the big ol' city. Don't worry, we'll show you how to really live it up on a Saturday night."

They exchanged smiles, and in only a few minutes alone in a car together, they didn't feel so much like strangers anymore. In fact, it felt like they had known each other for years.

"You ever go to the city?" she asked him.

"No, not really."

Valeria wanted to ask him why, but she was suddenly distracted by something. "Wait, you said *we'll* show you a good night, who's 'we'?"

Just as Valeria asked the question, the Bad Boy pulled up to the side of an empty road in front of some houses, and turned to her.

"Oh, a friend of mine – Lena, is gonna be with us tonight. When you called I had already made plans with her and I couldn't cancel, so I thought we could spend it altogether, that ok?"

A punch to the stomach for Valeria, as she realised suddenly that this was not a date at all. This was not even an evening just for the two of them. This was Valeria third-wheeling the Bad Boy and some girl.

She wondered why he had not mentioned this Lena girl before this moment, and something felt rather odd about it. As if she had been completely blind sighted.

"Sure," was all Valeria could say, and just as she began to process his words and the plan for the evening, the back door suddenly clicked opened.

A pretty girl with a bouncy ponytail and alarmed, big brown eyes hopped into the car and slammed it shut.

"Argh, I hate my parents! Drive, Leo! Drive, damn it! Before they fucking catch me!"

6

Marilyn Manson's 'Tainted Love' blasted from the speakers of the Bad Boy's car, as he sped down the dark roads of the mountainous countryside. Lena hummed to herself as she lit up a cigarette, and Valeria was silent, still taking in the arrival of the mysterious female stranger in the car.

"Fuck! Stop swerving, you gigantic asshole!" Lena yelled at the Bad Boy, which only made him proceed to swerve even more. "I hate you, you fucktard! You hear me?!"

Valeria couldn't help laughing at the way the female stranger yelled at the Bad Boy, as if he was an irritating ten-year-old kid she couldn't stand to be around. The Bad Boy joined in laughing as Lena continued to yell at him, and Valeria watched her as she slowly but surely coolly lit her cigarette in the backseat.

She watched her slick, black ponytail blowing in the wind, as she scrolled down both the back windows. The air was cold, even for summer, but that's what you got when you chose to holiday in the countryside in August. During the day it was sunny and hot, but come evening the mountains brought an eerily cold breeze to the night.

"I'm Lena," she yelled over Marilyn Manson, looking up at Valeria briefly before fixing her eyes back on her cigarette. She then ordered them both to open their windows and watched them obey. Lena had an authoritative element to her that made others listen. Even the Bad Boy.

Valeria applauded her playfully as she blew out a smoke ring that disappeared with the wind in exactly 0.5 seconds.

"Finally! Only took you a good half an hour!" the Bad Boy yelled over Marilyn Manson.

"Shut up, douchebag." Lena narrowed her eyes at Valeria, as she took a swig from her cigarette. "So," she began, as she blew out more smoke. "Leo says you're from the city? I have a friend that lives there – Eric! Hey!" she suddenly tugged at the Bad

Boy's leather jacket. "We should go visit him! And Valeria!"

Lena seemed like one of those naturally high people. She didn't need alcohol.

"What the fuck, Lena! I'm driving! Can you leave my jacket alone please?!" the Bad Boy shrugged her off, batting her hand away as if she were a fly.

Valeria watched them as they playfully argued and wondered how long they had been friends. Envy quickly filled her soul as she watched their strong rapport and understanding of one another unveil itself to her. It was as if the yelling and screaming at one another was their way of telling each other that they didn't mind each other's personalities. That they in fact loved each other's personalities.

Valeria couldn't help wondering if they had ever hooked up.

Kissed.

Had sex.

Spooned.

It looked possible, but at sixteen, Valeria wasn't exactly good at reading these things yet.

"Such a crabby twat! Asshole! You can drop me back home, you know!"

"Back to your crazy parents?! The ones that threatened to kick you out of the house?!" the Bad Boy pointed out.

Lena was silent for a moment as she blew out smoke with pensive eyes. "Okay maybe not," she looked out the window with a certain sadness. "Let's go get drunk."

"That's the plan. Valeria's never been out around here, and I don't think she's a partier back in the city either, given the look she gave me when I said Red Flags is only our first stop."

Lena's expression brightened, and she smiled at her. "What?! But you live in the city!"

"She's sixteen though, not the legal age to get into clubs there yet," the Bad Boy answered for Valeria.

"Ooh. Well you're in luck, here in the countryside nobody gives a fuck," Lena eyes suddenly lit up. "Oh, I'm going to introduce you to everyone. And we're going to get hammered. Mark my words! It's going to be a wild one!"

"Okay Lena, I still have to get her home in one piece, yeah?" the Bad Boy told her.

Valeria glanced at the Bad Boy, studying him curiously. She didn't understand him, and this only seemed to interest her more. On one hand, he was a Bad Boy, a rebel, a guy that didn't give a fuck about anything. And on the other hand, he was by far the only adult in the car.

It also seemed that he wanted to take her out and show her a good time, but that he also cared, and wanted to see no harm come to her. This, in turn, made Valeria feel safe around the Bad Boy pretty quickly. As if she knew he would always come to her defence. Not that she wanted that though, of course.

"I can take care of myself," Valeria told him coolly, despite the fear mounting at the pit of her stomach for what this sentence could mean for all three of them that night.

The Bad Boy stared at her curiously for a few moments, before pushing his foot down on the pedal and accelerating, his smile growing bigger.

They didn't take their eyes off each other, and Valeria didn't dare look away, nor flinch, nor show fear. She kept her eyes fixed on him as he continued to speed up, giving him her best poker face. She wouldn't even reach out to clutch the door handle. No matter how nauseous she felt.

I am not afraid.

I am not afraid.

I am not afraid...

"Let's get this party started then," the Bad Boy suddenly said, as he swerved round another mountain corner at full speed.

Both Valeria and Lena clutched their door handles tightly, Lena yelling profanities at the Bad Boy once more, as they made their way into the black of night.

7

"Drink up!" the Bad Boy ordered, and Valeria gulped down the shot in synch with Lena. They threw down their glasses with squeals, as the alcohol sizzled in their chests.

The Bad Boy shook his head, totally sober, as he swallowed his shot with ease, and wiped his mouth with the sleeve of his jacket. "You two are such lightweights."

"Your leather jacket saves you from the alcohol intake!" Valeria said, aware that her thoughts no longer made such sense, but unable to stop herself from sharing them with whoever was willing to listen.

As you can imagine for any sixteen-year-old who had never had a proper drink before, the alcohol had a rather immediate effect on Valeria, only truly needing one sip of her vodka and melon to find herself dancing the Macarena on the top of a bar table.

It was now three vodka and melons, one Amaretto, and two shots later, and things were getting bad for Valeria.

Her chest was burning and her head beginning to spin, but she wasn't going to let the others know that it was probably time to take a break. This would make her look weak, inexperienced, and naïve. And that's the last thing you want to be seen as when you're sixteen.

"It saves you, like a guardian angel!" Valeria added, as she giggled with Lena and the Bad Boy only raised an eyebrow at them with a small, amused smile. "So, where are we now?" she asked.

It was a justified question, given that this was their fourth or fifth bar and every location was starting to look the same.

It was past 3AM and Lena had so far introduced Valeria to essentially everyone they encountered, for there wasn't a soul in these bars she didn't know. Most of them were cute guys, but Valeria found them too boring to catch her eye. They usually stood there, awkward and tipsy, as their conversation skills severed and died in front of her.

That didn't seem to bother Valeria in the slightest however. After all, Valeria wasn't there to meet a guy, she was there to experience her first night out in the countryside, and to spend some time with the Bad Boy. Be it the alcohol, or the excitement of the evening, but Valeria found herself feeling more alive, and more human, than she had ever felt previously.

In fact she understood, for the first time in her life, why other sixteen year olds liked to go out on Saturday night – it was a way to let off steam, it was a way to have fun with the people that you liked, and it was a way to relax.

Valeria liked the Bad Boy, it was decided. And she had made this decision two hours into their Saturday night adventure.

Sure, he was the town rebel, but she was now convinced that there was more depth to him that Valeria had initially anticipated. As if underneath all that tough guy persona were layers and layers to him that Valeria wanted desperately to unveil, to understand, to get to know. There was more to him than caught the eye, and she was starting to think that perhaps he had a good heart after all.

He told good stories, he had a charismatic smile (though he rarely showed it), and he wouldn't let either of the girls pay for any of their drinks or food. In some thwarted way, there were elements of gentleman to the Bad Boy that Valeria found most intriguing and surprising.

He was passionate about three things: punk, politics, and people. He loved 70s punk the most – more specifically angry, bald men singing into the mic and not playing properly. His politics were complicating, but he was essentially one who wanted equal rights for everyone, and spoke a lot about racism and homophobia.

Lastly, he liked to study people. He read a lot of psychology books and even did a few tricks on Valeria – asking her to tell a story from her past, and when she turned her eyes to the right, he pointed a finger at her and said, 'ha! You searched your memory for that story, because the right side of the brain carries memory!'

Valeria understood pretty quickly that though the Bad Boy wasn't exactly a hardworking, driven young man, he had the intelligence to go really far.

If only he could shift his focus from drag racing and drugs.

Yes, the Bad Boy was a fan of both of these things, though he didn't personally bring them up. It was only from Lena's mouth that these passions were exposed to Valeria, whilst the Bad Boy kept his head down and smoothly changed the subject. Valeria tried to imagine the Bad Boy drag racing and she envisioned it with a cold, careless look on his face, as if he didn't care if he lived or died.

It was clear to Valeria that the Bad Boy was afraid of nothing.

"This is Joe's! Joe's Bar!" Lena wailed even though she was standing right next to Valeria; the girls had stopped speaking to each other at a normal decibel a couple of hours back.

Valeria wasn't sure she liked Lena yet. She was a little too vivacious for her to handle sober, and she seemed rather fake. You know, one of those girls who can give you the brightest, friendliest smile, but underneath, they're a sugar-coated mess and they don't like you at all. But when drunk, hell, Lena was a hoot to be around, and she equilibrated the brooding Bad Boy who could care less about parties and knowing everyone in town.

It was also obvious to Valeria, even without knowing him, that the Bad Boy was only participating in the evening's events and nodding politely at people to keep the girls in his company happy, and she appreciated this.

Valeria had of course given up on this being any sort of date between the Bad Boy and herself, now that Lena had gate crashed it. She was however having fun nonetheless, and she liked feeling as if Lena and herself were the Bad Boy's two favourite girls in the entire world.

"Val!" a manly voice suddenly said, and when Valeria turned around, it took her a few seconds to recognise the person standing before her, for he was now no longer a fifteen-year old kid, but a seventeen-year-old young man.

"Ben, is that you?!"

Ben and Valeria had met at a town gathering two summers ago, exactly one week before Valeria set her eyes on the Bad Boy for the first time at the volleyball tournament. They had shared fascinating conversations about grunge music and books, but had never swapped numbers. She had thought about him after that night, sure, but once she saw the Bad Boy for the first time, thoughts of Ben left her until this very moment.

"What are you doing here?!" Ben asked her, just as Lena mouthed 'we're going outside for a cigarette'.

Valeria nodded and briefly watched the Bad Boy and Lena walk out, before turning her attention back to the handsome man in front of her. He looked much older than his seventeen years and had grown up incredibly well.

"Here for the summer! How have you been?!" Valeria asked him, trying to stop herself from shouting everything drunkenly but failing miserably.

"Oh, that's great! Look at you, all grown up! Enjoying the party?"

Things were finally clicking into place for Valeria as she studied Ben. Her heart was racing and her libido awakening as she looked at Ben's chiselled jaw, blue-green eyes and wonderful smile.

I was always supposed to like Ben.

The Bad Boy was a distraction that at fourteen was nice, but Ben is by far my taste in men now.

Valeria wanted to talk to Ben, she did, she wanted to give him her full attention, to find out what he was doing now, to swap numbers and even go out sometime. But it was not the time, nor the place. She was there with the Bad Boy and Lena, and she would remain loyal to them. She may have been very attracted to the handsome man standing in front of her, but it was the Bad Boy and Lena that was with her that night, and she didn't want to betray them.

"You should come over to Dixy's, they're having an after party, we can catch up. I'm making my way, just looking for my brother..." Ben told her.

Valeria wanted to go, she did. She wanted to run out of there with this handsome Ben and start this new and enticing adventure that was being dangled in front of her.

Yet Valeria knew she couldn't. She was aware that the Bad Boy and Lena had played host to her all evening, introducing her to people, and feeding her drinks without accepting her money. She couldn't ditch them. It didn't seem right.

"I'm actually here with Leo and Lena, you know them?" Valeria asked.

"Yeah, I know them," he told her and though Valeria didn't know Ben very well, she *knew* that he was holding back calling the Bad Boy a severe troublemaker. They were clearly not friends.

"Sorry, Ben. But maybe another night? I'm here for the summer."

Ben nodded at her with that attractive smile of his, and Valeria made her way through the crowd to the gardens to see if she could find the Bad Boy and Lena anywhere.

Failing miserably, she decided to wait for them outside in the cold, surrounded by crowds of smokers.

"Did you find them yet?!" Ben asked, as he came out of the bar rolling a cigarette and his older brother, Michael, by his side.

"No, I'm just waiting for either of them to..." Valeria's voice died away, as she spotted something suddenly. She froze, mid-sentence.

It was the Bad Boy and Lena in the bushes, kissing.

Passionately.

Lovingly.

Groping each other's bodies as if they knew them well.

Smiling at one another as they kissed zealously.

It hit Valeria like a punch to the stomach, as she realised that she was the third wheel to a couple, that the Bad Boy hadn't ever asked her out, that all this time, they had both been lying to her.

And neither of them had thought to be honest with her.

Valeria was surprised at just how much this hurt her; it stung and continued to sting and she needed to do something quick. She needed to get out of there, because the jealousy and the pain of what she was seeing in front of her was angering her to no end.

She instantly turned around to face Ben and his brother.

"Where did you say this after party is?"

2014

8

Arriving back in the small town, Valeria realised that everything looked exactly the same as it had done two summers ago.

Set to turn eighteen very soon, Valeria was both happy and sad to be back. Happy because she would be able to hang out with Pattie, to breathe in the countryside air she had actually missed in these two years, and to have a break from her life.

Sad because, well, the last time she had been in that town, things had not exactly gone to plan.

She suddenly had flashbacks of the Bad Boy and Lena making out in the bushes and gulped. She remembered running out of the bar with Ben and his brother scurrying after her, feeling the sting of betrayal running through her veins for the very first time.

What followed was Ben and his brother dropping a very quiet Valeria home, where she proceeded to pack up her things and declare to her parents that she was heading out to stay with her aunt Patricia back in the city.

Meanwhile, the Bad Boy called Valeria repeatedly, and she ignored each and every call, and each and every message.

Until eventually, he stopped.

Valeria found out some time later from Pattie in casual conversation that the Bad Boy and Lena had been together for half a year already. As soon as she learnt this fact, she couldn't help remembering the way he had looked at her in Pattie's garden, so full of lust and desire and interest in her.

She wasn't exactly a relationship expert at sixteen, but she knew, at the core, that what he did, and how he had looked at her, were not actions of a (true) man in a relationship with someone else. She knew then that she wanted nothing more to do with him.

Even walking the pathway up to the entrance of Pattie's house pushed further memories to Valeria's mind. Memories she had spent the last two years repressing.

She re-lived the Bad Boy picking her up in his Audi that fateful night, the aftershave he had been wearing, the way his little sister had been sitting upfront with the mirror down as she did her make up, not a care in the world.

Valeria remembered how she had first thought the Bad Boy was nothing but an idiot, yet as soon as he had mentioned he had seen her walking through town, that he had noticed her, her guard had started coming down. She had started changing her mind about him.

What was that, anyway? Valeria found herself asking, as she approached Pattie's front door. *A guy tells you he saw you and you're ready to give him the benefit of the doubt?*

Well Valeria, you were sixteen and a virgin.

Things are different now.

Indeed, a lot had changed in two years. Valeria had graduated sixth form college, had gone on several dates, kissed several bad eggs, and eventually met a good egg, Wayne, who was now her boyfriend.

Wayne was the sweet lead guitarist of a rock band that were mildly famous back in the city, though virtually unheard of in the countryside, so Valeria didn't expect Pattie or any of the others to know the band.

Valeria liked Wayne enough to lose her virginity to him, to commit herself to him, and she was happy. Fulfilled. Settled. And her trip back to the small town was not going to change any of that. She was a girlfriend to someone for the very first time and she was taking it very seriously.

The front door suddenly flung open and Pattie stood there with a huge grin on her face.

"Oh my God, it's been too long!"

Before Valeria could even attempt to reply, Pattie pulled her into a tight hug. Valeria was back in the small town, and though there was not the usual detest and resentment for this town, there was one rather big difference: She was back there alone without her parents, who had decided to skip the town that summer and instead head to Tahiti. Valeria, however, had had an urge to return, to spend some time by herself, to understand the countryside better.

She was curious.

"We're going to do so much this summer! I have so many things planned for us, and there's some great food festivals in the mountains I'm going to take you to!"

Valeria smiled. To turn eighteen in this town, alone, had not originally been on the agenda, Wayne was supposed to be with her but had been called out on a last minute tour.

Valeria followed Pattie into the kitchen with a certain carefree strut, happy to see her and to hear all the latest gossip of her life, when she suddenly froze at what, or more, *who*, she saw in front of her.

There, at Pattie's kitchen table, sat the Bad Boy. He wore that same damn leather jacket from two years ago, though it now looked a little tired, a little worn out, but just as rebellious as it did back then.

The Bad Boy himself looked relatively the same, except his hair was longer and hung over his forehead in a sexy way, and his eyes were fixed on Valeria with all the focus he could muster.

It was obvious that the Bad Boy was glad to see Valeria, and though he tried really hard to mask the happiness, she could see it anyway – that joy. That relief.

As if he had waited two whole years for this exact moment.

"Hey Valeria," he said, his hand cupping the mug of tea sat in front of him.

9

"Hi," Valeria managed to say in a neutral tone, careful to not reveal her dislike for the Bad Boy to Pattie. On the inside however, Valeria was experiencing a myriad of colourful emotions – confusion, anger, disgust, all for the man sitting at the table in front of them.

She also felt extremely foolish, the same sort of foolish she had experienced when she had seen the Bad Boy and Lena making out in the bushes two years earlier. Foolishness for having not understood the situation sooner, for having thought the Bad Boy was honest in any way, shape or form. For having been so desperate to venture into the countryside nightlife that she had been willing to get into a car and drive to God knows where with a stranger that she *knew* was the Town Loser.

She had relied on Pattie's moral compass on that one, but hey, she had been sixteen. Nobody at sixteen knows that hippies trust everyone.

Valeria was so sure that after the Bad Boy had given up texting that he would simply leave her alone. Okay, she wasn't entirely sure that that would be the case, which was why she had stayed away for two whole years. But she had hoped he had forgotten her, that she could have a peaceful summer in the country without having to see him, or deal with him, or even remember him.

She had moved on with her life, found herself and also found love – the gorgeous Wayne, lead guitarist of Brandy Shoes. Valeria had moved on from even considering something romantic with the Bad Boy. In fact, seeing him had sparked no reaction in her whatsoever.

Okay that wasn't true, she was trembling pretty much straight away, and her palms had become instantly sweaty.

But she wouldn't for the life of her let it show.

"Leo dropped by to help me with some of my tax forms," Pattie said. "We've finished now, but I suppose you two will want to catch up!"

I think I would rather poke my own eyes out.

As Pattie poured some soup into a bowl and set it on the table, Leo and Valeria stared at one another in intrigue. She disliked the person in front of her so much, yet it still seemed to spark such a strong reaction in her to see him. Or perhaps it was just the shock.

"Right, there you are, Val! Come on, what are you doing over there?! Sit down and eat before it gets cold!"

Before Valeria could respond, Pattie's dog Sunset started barking from the back garden. "Sunset! Sunset, stop chasing the neighbour's cat!" Pattie yelled, informing the Bad Boy and Valeria that she'd be right back.

Before Valeria could think of a reason to join her that didn't seem completely absurd, Pattie was gone.

Suddenly alone in the kitchen together, the tension between Valeria and the Bad Boy only grew fiercer.

"You should eat it before it gets cold," the Bad Boy said with a slight smile, as he nodded at the plate of soup. As soon as Valeria heard his voice again, it sent goose bumps down her neck. More flashbacks from two years ago leapt to the front of her mind – gulping down shots together, Marilyn Manson songs blasting from his car as Lena tried blowing out smoke rings.

The smell of his car.

The Bad Boy's smile.

That one brief moment where Valeria and the Bad Boy had shared an intense stare in the darkness of his car.

Valeria decided to resist spurting out snide remarks and instead sat down opposite him.

"How was the train ride in?" he asked her, as he got up and scrolled up the kitchen window, his eyes not leaving her for a second.

"What are you doing here?" Valeria asked coldly, in-between spoonful's of tortellini soup.

Yum, I have missed this. Pattie really does make the best tortellini soup in the world.

"I'm helping Pattie with some council stuff."

"At 7pm on a Sunday night?" Valeria snapped.

"It's a good a time as ever, don't you think?" he studied her curiously. "How have you been?"

The question was said in a very serious tone, as if he really and truly wanted to know the answer.

You're not going to fool me this time.

You're not a brooding Bad Boy who secretly has a heart underneath all that rough.

You're not.

Instead you're the guy that hides the fact that he is in a relationship.

Before Valeria could reply, Pattie marched into the kitchen with Sunset scurrying after her, rambling on about how much she hated paying taxes and filling out all the tiresome forms just because she was a freelancer.

Valeria and the Bad Boy tried to hide the extremely obvious tension between them now, as they listened patiently to Pattie's rant, their eyes not leaving one another in fascination.

Pattie however was quick to leave again, rushing back out into the garden to retrieve Sunset's favourite toy.

"I'll keep you company as you eat, if that's ok," the Bad Boy told Valeria, and she didn't reply. Instead, she took another spoonful of tortellini soup, her phone buzzing in her jacket.

Wayne:

Missing you already, babe.

Wish I was there! Xx

Valeria smiled to herself, unintentionally, making it abundantly clear to the Bad Boy that there was a guy in the picture. Yes, finally there was someone in the picture for Valeria. She was off the market, and none of this was dangerous territory anymore.

The Bad Boy gulped, pretending not to see the smile, deciding instead to perch himself on Pattie's window sill, as he lit up a cigarette. He looked out at Pattie's garden with pensive eyes, a cigarette between his lips.

"How's Lena?" Valeria asked, and as soon as the words left her mouth, she realised just how bitter they sounded.

Come on Val, it's been two fucking years!

You have a boyfriend now.

You don't care what the Bad Boy does, or what he thinks, or who he's with.

Not anymore.

Though Valeria told herself these things, she couldn't deny that there was palpable sexual chemistry between them. She acknowledged that, despite his horrendous personality, she found the man in front of her attractive.

She didn't understand how that was possible, but that didn't matter, because she knew she could control it.

It didn't make a difference if there was sexual tension between them, if she wanted him to reach across the table and kiss him. It didn't matter if she wanted to strip off of all his clothes and kiss him everywhere. That she could imagine them naked in Pattie's kitchen in several positions.

And it didn't matter because she would never do anything to compromise her relationship with Wayne.

The Bad Boy smiled at the mention of Lena and the detection of bitterness in her tone, as if confirming for him something he hadn't been sure about for two whole years.

He scrolled down the window and kept his eyes fixed on Valeria as he did so. "Lena? You don't think we're still together, do you?! We broke up months ago!"

Valeria's heart quickly lit up and just as quickly sank, as she realised that this meant that they had been together for two whole years.

Wow.

Their gaze was broken only by Pattie walking back into the kitchen and sighing in exhaustion. "That dog is beyond tiring." She looked at them both and smiled, narrowing her eyes at Leo. "See Leo, told you she'd be back." She glanced at Valeria, nodding at the Bad Boy. "He's been asking about you constantly for two frekin' years. Like annoyingly so."

Valeria's heart warmed at this thought. She knew it was wrong, that the Bad Boy was not a very nice person, that she needed to stay away from him and not let her emotions get the better of her, but she couldn't help it. Warm feelings continued to consume her, to take over every inch of her.

And just as Pattie turned around to grab some soup for herself, the Bad Boy leaned in towards Valeria.

"Hey, after dinner can I drop you home instead of Pattie?" he whispered, just loud enough for Valeria to hear.

Say no!

Say no!

It's obviously a no.

I am staying away from him this summer.

This is extremely clear.

Just say it!

The Bad Boy watched Valeria remain mute, as she gulped down another delicious spoonful of tortellini soup. And though no one else in the room knew it, Valeria was secretly smiling on the inside.

10

The Bad Boy raced down the streets of the tiny town, and Valeria smiled coolly, as she clasped the door handle for support. They could hear her luggage rocking back and forth in the seat behind her every time he swerved, like a constant reminder that she had only just arrived back in town.

She had had no intentions of seeing the Bad Boy, yet three hours in, here she was, agreeing to let him drive her home.

It was a fifteen-minute walk and Pattie was supposed to take her, but he had insisted he do it, given they were practically neighbours and it was past 10pm.

At least, these were the reasons the Bad Boy had listed as they had sat in Pattie's kitchen. They were valid reasons in Pattie's opinion and Valeria found herself finding it hard to object.

Once alone in the Bad Boy's car for the first time in two years, they spoke briefly about Pattie's tortellini soup and how much they both loved it.

But that was it. Neither of them felt the obligation to always be talking, as if they were already incredibly comfortable around one another, even though they hadn't spent more than one evening together in their entire lives.

It was nuts.

"Valeria," the Bad Boy suddenly said, after a couple minutes of silence. "Lena and I... I'm sorry that we didn't tell you. It was still a secret relationship at the time because of her parents. It wasn't something navigated towards you in particular, and it wasn't done with spiteful or disrespectful intent.

I just wanted to see you that night, and I knew if I didn't find a way to make that happen, you wouldn't have agreed to go out with me on another occasion."

Valeria opened her mouth to object, but remained mute. She knew he was right. The only reason she had agreed to go out with him that night was because she had been stuck at Pattie's playing cards and she had been bored out of her mind.

She didn't know what to say, mostly because the sincerity in his words had warmed her in the most surprising way. It was, after all, the apology she had been waiting a whole two years for.

And so she said nothing, instead exchanging small smiles with him before he focused back on the road completely.

As he continued to speed through the town, Valeria spotted her parents' house in the distance, and they both tensed as Raw Power blasted from the Bad Boy's speakers. They kept their eyes fixed on the house in silence as the Bad Boy slowed down, and Valeria suddenly found herself wishing that the Bad Boy would just drive past it.

That he would just simply ignore her house, and make the decision for both of them that that evening was not going to end like this.

The truth was, the second Valeria had got into the Bad Boy's car and they were alone for the first time since their drive to Lena's two years ago, she suddenly didn't want to separate from him, or his presence.

There was something between them, an intriguing chemistry that sizzled, and kept Valeria glued to him. She hardly knew anything about him, yet she felt there was an atmosphere unique to only their presence, and she didn't want to let it go to waste with just a four-minute car journey to her house.

She wanted to spend more time with him, to talk to him, to catch up with him, even if it were to just drive around in silence. Because with him, and she understood this instantly, when they were alone, they were themselves. Completely and utterly themselves.

The Bad Boy suddenly picked up speed again, accelerating so fast that it pulled them both back in their seats. The Bad Boy drove straight passed Valeria's house, without saying a word. The silence between them went from comfortable to curious, as they embraced the synchronisation of their desires.

Valeria could not believe what was happening, how he was capable of reading her mind like this.

"Shall we get a drink?" he said to her nonchalantly, and Valeria felt her stomach go all giddy with excitement as soon as he asked the question.

"Okay," was the only word she could muster without giving away the excitement and nerves running around inside of her.

She glanced at the Bad Boy, who smiled slightly, as he kept his eyes fixed on the road. Valeria relaxed a little, resting her elbow on the window and lying back in her seat.

Well, this evening just got a hell of a lot more interesting...

11

"I'm telling you, the Vietnam War goes way back to 19th century French imperialism!" the Bad Boy exclaimed, clutching his beer with one hand and waving in Valeria's face with the other.

"Oh come on, you're telling me that the route cause actually happened an entire century earlier? How is that even possible?!" Valeria yelled back. "There might be brief elements of it, but not actual route cause!"

Valeria and the Bad Boy sat opposite each other in a rowdy pub in the next town, smiling at one another. They had been playfully arguing and discussing war and history for four hours straight.

They would occasionally stop to drink their drinks, or have a quick chat with the pub owner, Geoff, as he floated by. He was a nice man in his late thirties who lived alone upstairs. Of course, he had known Leo a long time and they chatted briefly. It seemed that the Bad Boy seemed to like him.

Valeria had not expected this sort of quality of conversation at all. She had expected to talk to the Bad Boy about the town, about their summers, even about their love lives maybe, but politics? War? History? Lena had mentioned two years ago that he was into politics, but Valeria didn't realise to what extent.

With every passing moment, she was learning more and more about him. The more this happened, the more her attraction to him increased. Their chemistry was only growing stronger. Every insult to one another, every playful sentence, it only brought them closer. They were both tough, and thick-skinned, and full of energy.

He was also incredibly funny, which was rather surprising to Valeria.

Who knew Bad Boys could be funny? She found herself asking.

Yet he *was* funny, and he had already made her laugh a handful of times that evening. And not pity laughter, but that sort of uncontrollable laughter that makes your stomach hurt.

Unknowingly to Valeria, this was something that the Bad Boy was striving for – to make her laugh. Because when she laughed, it made him smile. He liked to see her happy.

Perhaps the third Irish coffee was also contributing to Valeria's abundant laughter – the Bad Boy had introduced her to the drink only hours earlier and she had fallen instantly in love with it, so much so that she couldn't seem to stop drinking them.

She suddenly hit the table with her hand dramatically, as she giggled loudly. She was looking at something behind him and so the Bad Boy turned around to find her laughing at a group of guys who had just walked in. There was nothing particularly humorous about them, yet Valeria only continued to laugh.

"Alright," the Bad Boy said, "pace yourself with the Irish Coffees."

He smiled as he said it, studying every inch of her face with warmth in his eyes. That coldness that usually haunted his blue pupils was not currently present. She could feel that this was a rare side to him that not many people in his life got to see. She wondered why she was one of the lucky few to be allowed in, to see this version to him, why it felt like he trusted her, when they barely knew each other at all.

Feeling rather ballsy after gulping down the remainders of her third Irish Coffee, Valeria found herself asking the question she had wanted to ask him all night.

"So why did you and Lena break up? Two years is a pretty long time. Especially for people our age."

Valeria realised that she sounded much younger than someone who was about to turn eighteen in three days, but it was the alcohol. It always made her more of a child.

The Bad Boy sighed, looking down at his pint before locking eyes with her. His expression was the most serious she had ever seen it.

"We were good, and strong, and we decided at one point to move in together. But whilst I went out to work, she stayed home and watched cartoons all day. I'd come home and the kitchen would be dirty – I would have to clean it. I'd then have to make dinner. I was tired of being the only adult in the relationship."

Wow. Lena was silly to let this one go.

"She also didn't like me racing," he added. Valeria had forgotten that the Bad Boy was an illegal drag racer, something mentioned by Lena that night two years ago, but never uttered again.

"Why?" she asked.

"Because I was getting into a few accidents."

Valeria noticed that the Bad Boy couldn't even look her in the eye now and kept his head down on his beer. She could tell that the conversation was making him uncomfortable, almost fearful, yet she had to keep going, she had to get answers.

"Did you stop?" Her voice was lower now, and softer. As if approaching the topic with a lot more delicacy and consideration.

"I did for a while. Then we broke up. Then I got back into it," he looked up at her. "And it's going really great now, I love it." The happiness in the Bad Boy's eyes now made Valeria's worry shift to the side and be replaced with excitement.

Well if he's being careful and it makes him happy, what's the problem?

"Can I come out and see you race sometime?" Valeria asked, and she looked down at her empty glass with what appeared to be shame. "I've never even been on a motorbike."

"Erm, not sure that's a great idea, I mean– wait, *wait,* what?" the Bad Boy paused to read Valeria's embarrassed face. "You've never been on a motorbike before?!" His eyes were wide and shocked and excited, all at once.

Valeria shook her head, blushing, but the Bad Boy only smiled back at her.

"Well *this* we definitely have to change. As soon as possible," he told her, quickly gulping down the remainders of his beer, wiping his mouth with the sleeve of his leather jacket, and giving Valeria a particularly smug look.

Valeria's face dropped. "What, *now*?"

"Oh yes," he replied with a grin. "Now."

12

As the Bad Boy raced across the mountainous countryside in the black of night, Valeria was anything but scared. She was getting used to his fast driving, even enjoying it now.

She simply told herself that the lack of barriers on the roads didn't make a difference. If they were going to accidentally fly down a mountain, it was going to happen with or without that barrier. At least, according to Valeria.

She also decided that the song currently playing wasn't good enough to match her giddy and excited mood, and so she changed radio station.

Yet every song that blasted through the Bad Boy's speakers wasn't good enough for Valeria, not for the mood that she was currently in. She was about to go ride a motorbike for the very first time - she needed the very best. And so she continued to switch, and switch, and switch...

"Hey, will you quit that?!" the Bad Boy moaned, playfully.

"Nope!" Valeria giggled drunkenly, as her hair blew in the wind. She had opened both their windows, but it seemed to irritate the Bad Boy and he closed his.

Aware that the rapid radio station switching seemed to irritate the Bad Boy further, Valeria continued to do so, and he only looked at her.

"Jesus Christ, you're so annoying!" he told her, though he wasn't quite able to contain his smile as he said the words. A very tipsy Valeria knew that he found her anything about annoying, yet she loved to press his buttons.

If changing radio stations and opening their windows wasn't enough, she began sticking out her tongue at the Bad Boy, pretending to be a bee, the normal stuff that any sober person in the passenger seat would do.

"What are you doing?!" he asked her, biting his lip to stop himself from laughing. A Pantera song blasted from the speakers suddenly and Valeria left it there. She loved Pantera.

"Stop it!" he ordered, letting out a laugh.

"Never!" she replied, as she continued to disobey his requests.

When they arrived at the Bad Boy's family home, Valeria couldn't help but smile, having flashbacks of fourteen year-old her walking this street a hundred times a day, hoping to bump into him, to speak to him, to become a part of each other's lives.

As they got out of the car, the Bad Boy swore under his breath. "It's not here," he said, nodding at his empty drive way. "My cousin must have taken it out."

Valeria's stomach sank, as she realised she wasn't going to lose her motorbike virginity that night. She wasn't going to feel what it was like to ride a real motorbike, or to feel her body pressed up against the Bad Boy's.

Her phone suddenly buzzed a message.

Wayne:

I miss you! How's your first evening back in the small town going? Xx

Valeria was about to reply when the Bad Boy distracted her.

"You wanna see something cool?" he asked her, but he didn't stick around to hear Valeria's answer. Instead, he walked towards the backyard of his family home.

The Bad Boy's house was built on the top of a hill, with an incredible view of the surrounding mountains and gorgeous countryside beneath them. Valeria knew this view only from the official pathway that led down to the forest, a few houses down.

Valeria followed the Bad Boy, who was so focused it looked like he was in a trance. They walked the gravelled path past his bins, and turning the corner to his backyard. It took Valeria a few moments to understand that the Bad Boy was leading them into his neighbour's backyard.

"Hey! Where are you going?!" she hissed, starting to sober up as panic set in. "Hey!"

"Just want to show you something, come on," he said, at a normal decibel. Valeria wanted to argue, to demand that they go back, but she was too intrigued by what on Earth the Bad Boy could want to show her at 3am in someone else's backyard.

After they drunkenly climbed the fence, he stopped in front of a very large and opaque penn, and as Valeria tiptoed to see what was inside, she gasped as she spotted a Rottweiler sleeping. She jumped back, the way most people who weren't expecting to see a Rottweiler would.

The Bad Boy laughed a little at her reaction. "That's Megan," he told her. "Come here, Megan girl."

Why is he waking her?
What is he doing?
Is he nuts?!

Valeria's eyes widened as she watched the Rottweiler slowly wake up. She yawned, and seemed happy to see the Bad Boy. He leaned in, just as happy, and pet her head affectionately.

Valeria's panic was met with a strange joy to see them together like this. To see the Bad Boy happy. It was as if he trusted this dog a hell of a lot more than most humans.

They also seemed to really love each other.

"I've known her five years, trained her as a pup," the Bad Boy told her. "Then moved town and didn't see her too often as an adult."

Valeria continued to smile as she watched them together. She couldn't help feeling a little envious of Megan, who currently had all of the Bad Boy's attention and affection.

"Pet her, go on. She won't bite," he suddenly told her.

Valeria froze, her happiness for their reunion melting as the panic set in again.

"Uh, I'm okay," she told him, but she knew that as soon as he had asked, that he wouldn't be giving up on the idea quite so easily.

He smiled. "Come on, she won't bite. Trust me."

"I don't think-"

"Val. Trust me."

When Valeria looked into the Bad Boy's eyes, it was met with intense intrigue, and this only further intensified their chemistry.

Why are we here?

How did we end up here?

Is this normal?

Valeria was confused, and she felt her heart thumping through her chest. And she realised, as she looked at the Bad Boy, that she did trust him.

She didn't quite know when it had happened, or how, but it was there. She felt safe around the Bad Boy, as if he'd never put her in danger. As if he'd never let anything happen to her.

And so without saying a word, Valeria slowly and nervously reached into the penn with her hand.

Luckily for her, instead of biting Valeria's fingers right off, Meghan welcomed the affection.

"There you go," the Bad Boy said with a smile. Valeria wanted to ask him why this was so important to him, she wanted to tell him that Meghan's fur was a lot softer than she had imagined.

There were so many things that she wanted to say, but before either of them could, they suddenly heard noises in the house of the garden they were currently trespassing in.

The pair turned around to see the lights in the house switching on.

"Who's there?!" said a croaky, masculine voice.

"Shit, run!" the Bad Boy hissed, and they instantly bolted out of the garden, whispering their goodbyes to Meghan as they drunkenly laughed and stumbled across the garden.

13

Valeria stood in front of a huge lake in the darkness of the countryside with two friends, just as the clock struck midnight. Well, Robbie, her friend from the next town, was with her and he had brought with him his lovely girlfriend, Charlene, whom Valeria had never met before.

She was having a good time, she was. They were lovely; they bought her ice cream and drove her out to this beautiful lake for a mini picnic.

However, Valeria knew deep down that she wanted more from her 18th birthday. She didn't know what exactly, but she knew this wasn't the 18th birthday she had always wanted for herself. Yet she also knew it would be ungrateful of her to truly accept these thoughts and feelings. I mean, she was in the countryside without her boyfriend, her parents, or her friends, and she had chosen this.

So she just needed to be okay with what was offered to her. It was, after all, a lovely lake, and she was in good company.

Valeria decided to spend a good few minutes in front of the lake, contemplating where her life was headed now that she was, to society, a fully fledged adult. She did so as Robbie and Charlene chased each other around in the grass, giggling. It was nice to see Robbie happy.

When her phone buzzed a text, it took Valeria all of 0.5 seconds to pull out her phone to see who it was.

Wayne:

Happy birthday, my love! Hope you're having a good time with Robbie and Charlene :) xxx

Valeria smiled at the message, but it soon faded as she realised she had been craving a birthday message from someone else. Someone who lived much closer. Someone who knew it was her birthday, because she had mentioned it to him by purpose.

Someone she had been constantly texting since their night of drunken adventure that involved petting a Rottweiler.

She had flashbacks of the way they had looked at each other in the darkness of his neighbour's garden.

She remembered how happy she felt whenever she hung out with the Bad Boy. There was goodness to him, she felt it. And she wanted to see him, to hang out again, to be around each other.

Yet despite texting constantly since that night three days earlier, he had said absolutely nothing that entire evening, on the eve of her 18th birthday.

Valeria tried to push the Bad Boy to the back of her mind, and reminded herself that she had a boyfriend back in the city. A boyfriend that kept telling her how much he missed her and couldn't wait to see her. She knew she was very lucky to have him.

When Robbie and Charlene eventually dropped Valeria back home, the sadness was mounting. It was 1AM on her 18th birthday and she was already home, already going to sleep.

She dumped her bag on the bed, her phone on the nightstand, and tied her hair in a bun. She sighed in misery, as she tried to decide what song to listen to during her shower.

Just as Valeria decided it was going to be The Cure's 'Lullaby', her phone suddenly buzzed on the nightstand.

The Bad Boy:

Hey. How was your night?

She smiled at the sight of his name on her screen, and quickly typed back.

Valeria:

It was okay, nothing special. Yours?

The Bad Boy had told Valeria earlier in the day that he was going to drive down to a town a couple of hours away with some friends for some party.

The Bad Boy:

Nothing special.
Actually, it was quite boring.

Valeria's smile grew wider. She was glad the Bad Boy had had a bad time, that his evening had gone just as pathetically as hers.

Just as Valeria began to reply, she saw the Bad Boy typing.

Bad Boy:

Look outside.

Valeria froze as her eyes widened.

He can't be here?!

Did he drive back early?!

She rushed over to the window and it took only a few seconds to spot him across the road, and he wasn't alone – he was leaning against an incredibly beautiful motorbike.

Valeria gasped, as she took in everything she was seeing – the Bad Boy, his sexy leather jacket, the motorbike. The sight of it all covered her in goose bumps instantly.

He didn't smile or wave as they spotted each other, he instead dropped his eyes back to his phone to text, like the cool and collected Bad Boy that he was.

Bad Boy:

Come out. Let's go celebrate your 18th in style.

The 'OK' Valeria wrote in response to his invitation was the quickest 'OK' she had ever typed via text message in her entire life. She grabbed her stuff and headed out, meeting him at the porch. As soon as they were at a metre distance they both tensed, their usual chemistry hitting them in one big wave.

"Hi," the Bad Boy said, and Valeria could have sworn she saw a slight excitement in his eyes. "Ready to celebrate turning eighteen?"

Valeria grinned at the Bad Boy. He had planned it all, and who knew how long he had been waiting outside her house. "Sure. Where are we going?"

This is it.

I'm going to ride a motorbike.

For the very first time.

On my 18th birthday.

With the Bad Boy.

"Well if I told you that, the element of mystery would be ruined," the Bad Boy said, matter-of-factly, and he handed her the spare helmet. It was surprisingly heavy, and it was only then, as she nearly dropped it, that Valeria realised that she was trembling.

"Here," he told her, as he spotted Valeria struggling to put it on. Affectionately, he pulled the helmet over her head for her, and latched it up for her.

Their eyes remained on one another as he buckled her up, curiously watching each other as Valeria wondered what the hell she was getting herself into.

It was scary and exciting all at once, yet what Valeria felt the most was that this moment had been something she had both been waiting a whole four years for.

Valeria glanced at the huge and intimidating motorbike, before climbing it in order to get to the seat, and she managed to do so without the Bad

Boy's help. She felt secretly proud of her achievement, and waited in glee as the Bad Boy followed at the front.

"Hold onto my waist," the Bad Boy told her, and it was more an order than a request. She obeyed, awkwardly wrapping her arms around him and blushing as she felt how toned his chest was.

He started the engine. "Hold on tight!" he barked, and before Valeria could even think of a response, they were racing off into the mountains, and into the cloud of possibility that came with turning eighteen.

14

"Are you gonna be okay standing up?!" the Bad Boy asked Valeria, and she laughed, drunkenly.

"Of course I am, what are you talking about?!"

However, as soon as Valeria stood up from the barstool, she felt instantly dizzy and nauseous at the same time. The room began spinning, and she lost her balance.

"Woah!" the Bad Boy said, catching her just in time, and pulling her upright again. Their eyes remained on one another, as his hand held her lower back.

Chemistry, so much chemistry between us...

"What's happening?!" Valeria asked, as she sat back down and gripped the bar, cautiously.

"Well, dearest Val, this is you losing your beer virginity."

It was true - this was the first time Valeria had ever tried beer. Sure, she had tried wine, Martini,

Amaretto, but beer had never appealed to her; she just didn't like the taste. She was however in the countryside with her alcohol selection being very limited, and so she had decided to go with beer.

It was turning out to not be the greatest decision in the world.

"I'm not drunk, I'm not! I didn't even have that many!"

She began counting in her head: One, two, three, four...

The Bad Boy grinned at her – it was one of those rare childlike grins that he only shared with the world when he was a) truly comfortable with the other person, and b) tipsy.

Valeria used her fingers to count the amount of beer bottles she had drunk, but gave up at five, giving the Bad Boy a frustrated look.

"I don't even like beer!"

"Well tonight would prove otherwise," he replied, as he took a swig from his bottle. Valeria watched him intensely, as he looked around at the packed bar. She didn't understand how she could enjoy his company so much and not have anything in common with him. He was into motorbikes, illegal drag racing and was way more of a history buff than she was. Yet they never seemed to be able to shut up.

"How's the birthday girl?!" yelled a stranger, as he passed them.

"Fabulous, just fabulous!" Valeria replied, having no clue who he was.

The Bad Boy kept his eyes on her in curiosity as he got out a cigarette. "Enjoying your night?" he asked.

"I am actually," was Valeria's response, and she meant it. Their motorbike ride into the night turned out to be both relaxing and exciting at the same time for Valeria.

The Bad Boy had driven slow by purpose and she knew it, but she was grateful for this. Valeria wasn't quite sure she could quite handle motorbike racing just yet.

They had shortly arrived at this unknown bar just before 2AM, ordered beer after beer and spoken about anything and everything.

Some time after 3AM, the entire local football team had strolled in, celebrating their victory from earlier that night. The Bad Boy knew them all, plus the bartender, and had made them all sing happy birthday to Valeria.

Being sung happy birthday to by an entire football team – what more could a girl want for her 18th?

It was past 4AM then, and just as Valeria and the Bad Boy smiled at one another, she noticed someone familiar walk into the bar and order a beer. Valeria's eyes widened and she suddenly became uncomfortable. She looked anywhere but in his direction, and she hoped and prayed he wouldn't notice her.

Fuck, what is he doing here?

Valeria didn't want any trouble and so she continued as normal, listening to the Bad Boy talk to some guy about his sex life.

"....and then there was Martha, who you dropped for Susie, and then you dropped Susie for Hazel, am I right?"

The man jokingly swore at the Bad Boy, and he jokingly swore back. Everyone in the bar was pretty drunk by then, and conversations were beginning to not make much sense.

Valeria debated asking the Bad Boy if they could leave, but she was having too much fun. She didn't want to leave because of him. Plus, she wasn't sure how she would explain it to the Bad Boy.

She suddenly heard the bar stool next to hers drag across the floor as someone sat down. She knew, without looking, that it was him, and she knew, that trouble was coming,

"Hey Val, I didn't know you were back?" his voice was sinister and sent goose bumps down Valeria's neck.

"Yes, I am," was her blunt reply, hoping and begging that he would just leave her alone.

"So how long are you in town for?" he asked.

"Not long," she replied, again bluntly.

"Visiting alone?"

"Hey Wes, I know you haven't had sex in a few years, but can you back off?" the Bad Boy suddenly snapped.

Wesley Prim was a name Valeria knew well. She had first encountered him at age sixteen, when he followed her out of a bar and asked for her number. When she said no, he had told her he was going to rape her.

The second time they met, Wesley spotted Valeria at a bar in the next town. This time he followed her all around the bar, hounding her for a blow job.

Wesley Prim was, in short, the town perv. And Valeria was terrified of him.

"Get a life Leo, you have a girlfriend anyway - Sandra, remember?" Wesley replied.

A swift punch to the stomach for Valeria, as she turned to the Bad Boy with shocked eyes.

He has a new girlfriend?

He's not single?

But he just broke up with Lena some months ago?!

He's already got another one?

How much of a player is this guy?!

And why didn't he tell me?!

Alarm bells went off in Valeria's head – big ones, but before she could say anything, she felt an aggressive arm wrap around her waist. It was Wesley's.

"Come here baby, I'll show you a good time. City boys got nothing on me..."

"Get off me!" Valeria shouted rather loudly, as she attempted to slither out of his slimy clutches.

As she fought and struggled with Wesley, the Bad Boy was up in only a matter of seconds and throwing a punch at the pervert.

Wesley flew to the floor instantly, his hand leaving Valeria's waist. She squealed in shock as blood rushed from his nose, and all eyes in the bar were now on them.

"What the hell is going on here?!" the bartender, Bernie, yelled, as people backed away in shock.

Valeria knew they had to get out of there and fast, and so she attempted to slide out of her seat in her drunken state, but the beer consumption was too much for her to fight against. As if reading her mind, the Bad Boy heaved her over his shoulder in an instant and sprinted out of the bar.

"I'm gonna throw up!" Valeria wailed. Each step he took was a nauseating bounce to the upside down world that was currently her view.

"No you're not!" he put her down on the motorbike, hopped on at the front, and in only a few seconds, they were off.

Some of the footballers stepped outside with beers in their hands to see them off; baffled, drunken expressions on their faces as they watched on.

"Happy birthday!" one of them shouted, and it echoed again and again through the silent town.

Valeria was nauseous and confused at what had just happened, yet she managed to smile and grip the Bad Boy's chest with much more ease than when the evening had begun, for she had never felt safer...

15

"Here," the Bad Boy said, handing Valeria a can of unheard of German beer. "Had them in my car," he explained, as he took a sip from his can. "They've been there all evening but should be fine."

The pair stood at the window pane of Valeria's living room, looking out at the small town. It was 5AM by then, the sun was beginning to rise, and they had been standing at that window pane for a good few minutes in comfortable silence.

Following the events back at the bar, Valeria had finally calmed and was no longer trembling. The journey to her house had been in silence, as they both attempted to take in what had happened. Valeria hadn't thrown up on the way, which was surprising to her.

She took a sip of warm beer from the can and cringed up her nose at him.

"I know, I know, you'd think German beer would taste better," the Bad Boy told her. Before Valeria could respond, they noticed a lorry pull up on the other side of the road, exactly in front of the town bakery. They watched in silence, listening to the engine purr to a standstill.

"Every morning, at 5AM sharp. This guy is never late," the Bad Boy said. The pair of them watched the driver – fortysomething and bearded with a cap, he leapt out of the lorry, and made his way into the bakery.

The Bad Boy looked at Valeria. "You hungry?"

"Actually yes, come to think of it I am. What is open round here at this time though?"

The Bad Boy gave Valeria a cunning smile, as if she were missing a piece of the puzzle. "Do you like croissants?"

Her eyes grew bigger, as she realised what he was insinuating. "No way! You cannot be serious?! We'll get caught! And I'm pretty sure I run like a penguin right now!"

"Well then it's good that I was thinking that I go get them then. Chocolate or plain?"

"Hey, no-" but Valeria's efforts to stop the Bad Boy were futile – he was already out the door. She chased after him to try and stop him, but he was too fast for her. And so she ran back to the window nervously, and he drunkenly stumbled into view.

He waved at her excitedly, like a child on their way to get ice cream, and Valeria giggled, waving back. There was a surge of excitement, of adrenaline for Valeria as she watched it all unfold.

The Bad Boy now had this mischievous, childlike expression on his face, like a kid breaking into the headmaster's office, as he looked at Valeria. His keys jiggled in his back trouser pocket, as he drunkenly waddled over to the back of the lorry.

He pulled the back door down (everything was of course unlocked as it was the countryside), and Valeria cringed at the loud noise it made as he did so.

The Bad Boy disappeared into the lorry, as Valeria looked on with an intense gaze, making sure the driver didn't come back out of the shop. The quiet of the small town only added to the tension that Valeria felt in her stomach, who thought that if the driver did come back out, she would run over and distract him so that the Bad Boy could get away.

No way was she going to let him get in trouble for this.

The Bad Boy suddenly popped out of the lorry armed with croissants, and a huge sigh of relief hit Valeria as she watched him quickly close the door.

He gave Valeria the thumbs up and drunkenly stumbled out of view. She heard the front door open and rushed over, giggling with excitement.

"This is so awesome!" she yelped, and he held up four croissants with a grin.

"Chocolate, apricot or plain?"

She laughed. "I don't know, which one is your favourite?"

"I don't eat croissants. They're for you."

"What?!" Valeria blurted out, and she watched the Bad Boy put down the croissants on the table with a proud grin on his face in being able to feed her.

The pair drank more of the awful German beer as Valeria ate all four croissants with a hunger she hadn't felt in a long time, as they laughed at each other's embarrassing stories from childhood. The ridiculously loud laughter from both parties was partly the alcohol consumption, and partly because the pair seemed to have so much fun when they were together. As if they could be both serious and complete children in each other's company.

It was an hour later that they began to mellow down and feel a little sleepy. Valeria lay on the sofa now, her legs on the Bad Boy's lap. She thought about how scarily natural their bodies relaxed around one another, and never wanted to separate.

"So you have a girlfriend," she finally said.

The Bad Boy took a deep breath in. "Yes, I do. We met just after Lena and I broke up." There was silence between them, as Valeria took in this information. "What about you? Pattie tells me you have a boyfriend."

"I do - Wayne. Going on a year; he's nice."

"I don't really see you with someone 'nice'," the Bad Boy declared, matter-of-factly.

Valeria didn't say anything in response. Somehow she couldn't argue with him, she couldn't defend Wayne. So there they lay, two so-called friends, on a sofa together at sunrise.

Yet there was something strangely treacherous about what they were doing.

The Bad Boy slowly slipped horizontally on the sofa, resting his head on Valeria's stomach, and she ran her fingers through his hair.

She relaxed and smiled at the ceiling, as they both began to fall asleep.

And all she could think was, *this is the most perfect 18th birthday a girl could ever ask for...*

2015

16

When Valeria arrived back in the small town exactly one year later, a big part of the reason for her return was to see the Bad Boy.

The allure towards one another, and the unexplainable curiosity to their friendship was growing. She had known she wanted him in her life the first time she had seen him at the volleyball match back when she was fourteen; that desire to know him, to have him around her pulled and tugged at her since that very first time she had laid eyes on him.

Her soul had screamed for her to meet that person, somehow, some way. And it had taken them five years, but they had finally done it. They had finally developed a friendship.

Nineteen-year-old Valeria smiled at the sight of the Bad Boy as he walked up the path to the entrance of the bar. He looked exactly the same as he had done a year ago, and Valeria had flashbacks of her 18th birthday the previous year.

After spending the rest of the summer together, they had spent the entire year texting each other at least a couple of times a month. Valeria broke up with Wayne as soon as she returned to the city that summer, having understood that she didn't love him.

She had then spent most of the year buried in books for her second year of university, and the Bad Boy had started most of their text conversations during the course of the last year, just checking she was still alive.

It wasn't that she didn't think about him – she did, a lot. She just had a really busy year at university.

"Right on time," Valeria told him coolly, trying her best to remain casual. Trying to act as if she hadn't waited all year for this moment.

Yet she couldn't seem to pretend any longer, and her steps toward him began to accelerate, until she was practically bouncing, and she threw her arms around him. "Hi!"

"Hey, you."

It was Valeria's first night back in town and he had driven back early from work to shower, change and have a beer with her. They had chosen the bar they had visited the first time they had gone out together the previous year – Geoffrey's.

They spent another wonderful evening catching up on a year's worth of events, realising that a lot had changed since the last time they had seen each other.

For one, Valeria was slowly realising that after university, she had no idea what she was going to do with her life.

The Bad Boy was working odd jobs to afford his new flat a few towns away, and Valeria, as always, encouraged the Bad Boy to go back to school and choose a degree and a career he could truly love. He always laughed it off and politely disagreed with her suggestion. He was now single.

Valeria was also single, having not dated anyone seriously for the entire year. She sometimes thought about that night when the Bad Boy and herself had fallen asleep on the sofa and asked herself if it had meant something romantic.

To Valeria, it didn't feel quite platonic – the idea of the Bad Boy's head resting on her stomach, her fingers coming through his hair, but when these thoughts came into her mind she always dismissed it as nothing. And anyway, the fact that he hadn't even attempted to make a move that night made it that much more alluring, that much more enticing. And Valeria had decided, after a year's worth of thoughts, that the Bad Boy didn't like her, but that she perhaps liked him. Just that little bit.

It was a good seven hours later that they drunkenly stumbled out of the bar as it was closing, laughing at God knows what as Valeria linked arms with him. Geoff, the bar owner, bid them goodnight and they heard the door shut behind them.

Valeria and the Bad Boy hobbled down the path to the road and came to a halt on the pavement at the same time, both of them looking out at the beautifully quiet town. Not a sound could be heard and it was pure bliss.

They were supposed to call it a night there; Valeria's house was a two-minute walk from the bar and they had already made plans for the following day.

Yet they didn't call it a night. They continued to chat and chat, about silly stuff, about serious stuff, about random stuff, as time continued to pass, with neither of them making their way home.

They eventually walked across the road to the Bad Boy's car, where they were supposed to say goodbye, but they didn't.

And even when they stopped talking, they couldn't seem to leave each other's presence.

An hour later, things were a lot quieter. They had both mildly sobered up, and Valeria now sat in the driver's seat of the Bad Boy's car with the door wide open, the Bad Boy on the pavement, smoking a cigarette and checking something on his phone.

A punk rock song played at a low volume in the background, and Valeria bopped her head to it as she fiddled with the Bad Boy's knuckle brace.

She suddenly heard rustling in the forest across the street from them and instantly lowered the volume.

"What was that?" she asked, and the Bad Boy turned to her, confused. "I heard something in the forest," she added.

"Probably deer, they run free there and come out to play at this hour."

Valeria looked curiously at the Bad Boy. Never in all the years that she had visited the town had she ever come across any deer. There had never been any road signs either.

"*Deer?!* Don't bullshit me; I know better. There's no deer in this town," Valeria told him, matter-of-factly.

The Bad Boy's eyes smiled at her. "You don't believe me?"

"It's not deer, Leo."

"Fine, I'll show you!" the Bad Boy declared, flicking his cigarette to the ground and stamping it with the heel of his shoe.

"Fine!" Valeria jumped out of the driver's seat and watched as the Bad Boy got into the car, slamming the door, and starting the engine. Though fuming, Valeria froze now, trying to take in what was happening.

The Bad Boy gave her a childlike, almost innocent grin. "You scared, Val? Of the countryside?"

But as Valeria heard the question, she realised she wasn't afraid at all, because when she was with the Bad Boy, she never felt braver.

Her expression turned confident and she gave him a cunning smile. "What's the matter, Leo? Afraid I'll find out how full of shit you really are?" she said to him with a look of deviance in her eyes that he had never discovered before, and his grin only grew wider.

Valeria ran over to the passenger side and got in, as the Bad Boy raced off into the depths of the forest...

17

Valeria had never been particularly afraid of forests; she hadn't cried or hidden behind the sofa when she had watched The Blair Witch Project as a teenager. She didn't run away in fits of tears when she walked through the forest as a child with her parents, or even as an adult when she felt like going mushroom picking by herself. The forest had always been a beautiful, inspiring, and therapeutic place to Valeria.

However, she realised as the Bad Boy drove them both further into the depths of the woods, that she was now terrified of them.

It wasn't bright, inspiring and therapeutic anymore. At 4AM, forests were only eerie, unnerving, and as if something was constantly watching you.

The Bad Boy drove slow with his headlights on, the tyres running along the gravelled path, and the occasional low-hanging branch hitting the windshields.

An owl cooed in the distance, and there were rustles constantly being heard in the nearby bushes.

Valeria was essentially terrified, yet she was stubbornly hiding it behind big grins and useless small talk. She didn't want to show the Bad Boy that she was scared, that this was something new to her.

In part because she wanted to be fearless around him, but in part also because it was a strange type of fear, one she had never felt before. It blended with adrenaline, and excitement, to see where exactly they were heading. So though she knew she could turn to him at any moment and ask to go home, she didn't want to.

Because she trusted the Bad Boy. She felt safe with him. Even when they were driving through a forest at 4AM.

"Ah yes, I see many deer!" Valeria told him, sarcastically.

"You will, trust me," he said, with a grin. The Bad Boy was happy, excited, like a little child, and this warmed Valeria's heart to see. He was usually so serious, so cool, so Bad Boy.

"Is this all a plan to kill me?" Valeria joked, but as she said the words, she realised that if he wanted to, he could do it and nobody would ever know. Though the pub owner, Geoff, did see them leave together, the Bad Boy could cover his tracks impeccably well, she was sure of it.

Local police would write it off as her being eaten by a wolf, and nobody would ever know the truth.

The Bad Boy looked over at Valeria as he drove with one hand. "Yes Val, that was exactly my plan."

The pair of them smiled at one another as if under a spell. They couldn't take their eyes off one another, nor did they want to. Their gaze continued for a good minute and was only broken when Valeria suddenly noticed something on the road.

"Stop!" she yelled, and the Bad Boy instantly pulled on the brakes, heaving them forward.

They gawped, as they watched the deer in the middle of the road. He or she looked directly at them with its innocent, scared eyes.

"A deer in headlights," Valeria eventually said after at least ten seconds of shocked silence shared by the pair. "There's deer in this forest," she said, matter-of-factly and with disbelief in her tone. "All these years that I've been coming here..." her voice died away, as she continued to stare at the deer, and the deer looked back at her.

"Damn, I should have made a bet with you about this," the Bad Boy said. "You know, since I was right."

"Hmm," Valeria replied, still in awe of the deer in front of her.

"Say it then."

Valeria turned to the Bad Boy, confused. "Say what?"

"Say that I was right."

Valeria gave him a look of outrage. "What? Are you five?"

"Yes. Say it."

"No!"

"Val. I will never steal a croissant for you ever again or take you to see deer ever again if you don't admit your defeat."

"No!" Valeria squealed.

"I will get out of the car right now and scare the living shit out of this deer if you don't admit defeat!" the Bad Boy announced, and as Valeria sat in silence, he clicked open his door.

"No!" Valeria suddenly yelled, grabbing hold of his arm and pulling him back into the car. As their bodies touched, electricity struck them both. It was hard for them to focus on anything else when their bodies were touching.

It was pure and utter magic.

It was beyond any sort of chemistry neither of them had ever felt in their entire lives.

"Say it! Say it or I'm going to do it!" the Bad Boy managed to say, as Valeria giggled in a blend of nerves and excitement.

"No!"

"Say it!"

"No!"

"Say it!" the Bad Boy pulled away from Valeria's clutches and managed to get the door open a little wider so he could get out. Just as the Bad Boy was stepping out and away from her clutches, Valeria gave in.

"Fine! Fine! You were right! *You were right!*" she yelled in defeat, and the Bad Boy froze in his footsteps with a cunning smile on his face. "You're an asshole," she told him, and she moved back to her seat.

"Yeah, well, I was right."

"Soak it up, because you're never going to hear those words come out of my mouth ever again," she told him, "can we please now get out of here, in reverse, to not scare the deer."

"In reverse? Val, what do you take me for, some sort of pro driver?"

They smiled at each other as the Bad Boy slowly closed his car door. They took a few seconds to recover from all the contact they just had, before the Bad Boy eventually put his keys in the ignition.

He began to reverse them out of the forest in silence, though it didn't feel at all like they were going backwards.

18

The Bad Boy handed Valeria the spare helmet, and nineteen-year old Valeria eagerly put it on. She had been back in town just over a week and this was their third time hanging out since she arrived.

This was however their first motorbike ride together since her 18th birthday.

There was a nervous tension in the air as Valeria strapped on her helmet. He had text her asking her if she wanted to go for a 'real motorbike ride' and she had immediately texted back 'YES!'

She had, after all, waited years for this.

Valeria thought she was ready when she wrote that 'YES!', she really did, but she was beginning to feel more nervous than excited about the idea.

The Bad Boy had been in two major motorbike accidents in his life so far. Both had involved emergency surgery. The Bad Boy lived on the edge – that's just who he was. Was Valeria really ready to feel what it would be like to race? To put her life on the line like that?

Noticing that Valeria was struggling with her helmet, the Bad Boy walked over to her and gently pulled her hands away, strapping up her helmet for her. Sparks flew between them as soon as they touched, as always.

She studied his eyes through their helmets as he strapped her up, but she couldn't read him. He only looked like a typical Bad Boy – infinitely tough and desolate.

Am I really ready for this, when I haven't even learnt how to strap on a damn helmet?

But it was too late to debate it now. The Bad Boy got on first, and Valeria hopped on at the back. She grabbed hold of his chest before he had even started the engine, and he looked back at her. "Hold on tight throughout, okay?"

She nodded, nerves flooding her stomach.

No, stop, don't start to get nervous. He's a pro, remember?

Yet all Valeria could see were the stitches on his arms that he had shown her one night at the bar. He had spent two months in hospital.

The engine roared, and they *vroomed* off into the black of the countryside. He didn't waste any time picking up speed down the stranded streets of the small town, and they were instantly riding along at a comfortably fast pace.

This isn't scary at all, Valeria thought to herself. *This is fine! Why are people afraid to race?!*

Yet just as she had this thought, the Bad Boy turned the corner to a dark, long straight road where hardly any lampposts were working. It seemed to lead to nothing but infinite darkness.

The Bad Boy suddenly accelerated and only continued to do so. Valeria felt the engine in her stomach, and their bodies flying into nothingness.

As he continued to accelerate, they were suddenly going so fast that Valeria could no longer look around at their surroundings as they made her dizzy.

She held on tighter to the Bad Boy, as she closed her eyes, but that only made it worse, and so she quickly opened them. Even through the helmet, her mouth was drier than it had ever been.

They were going so fast that Valeria didn't even feel like she was in her own body anymore. She was a dot, flying through time.

She imagined them dying in several different scenarios; crashing into a tree, into a car, into a lorry. She remembered the Bad Boy's first accident at sixteen, the second one at nineteen. He had told her all the details of both horror stories and she heard his voice in her head, telling her every single thing about both traumas.

She now imagined both of them lying half dead in a ditch, and then in a hospital.

Valeria was terrified, more terrified than she had ever felt in her life, but she was flying too.

The Bad Boy continued to accelerate, and she continued to grip his hard chest with trembling hands. It felt as if they were going as fast as light itself, and yet simultaneously standing really still.

She didn't understand it, and her entire body was now trembling.

She began breathing heavily, ready for death. Ready for pain. Ready for the end. She would die before she would shout 'stop!' and she did not understand why. Why she wanted to keep going, despite the fear. Despite the atrocious feeling it gave every inch of her body.

She hated it, every moment of it. And yet, she loved it too.

Valeria noticed that they were starting to slow down, and he came to a stop at the entrance of the town's forest. The one where they had gone searching for deer just a few days earlier.

She got off, her legs completely jelly, and walked onto the grass to the side of the road in a zig-zag line. Having never felt like this in her entire life, Valeria quickly took off her helmet and kneeled over, waiting to be sick.

When nothing happened – nothing at all, she stood up straight and turned around to face the curious Bad Boy.

She wanted to speak, she did. She had wanted to tell him so many things – how she had hated it and loved it at the same time, how she had thought they were going to die, how that was the closest she had ever felt to flying.

But she couldn't. She was still in shock. She was still trembling and feeling nauseous.

Yet, when Valeria looked at the Bad Boy, she realised suddenly that they had something in common. That they had always had something in common. For as she looked at him, Valeria saw that they both loved to race for the same reason. And the Bad Boy could see it too, though he would never let it show.

Instead he smiled, and shook his head. "You realise you were holding my chest so tight that I was finding it hard to breathe, right? That's the only reason I stopped."

Valeria managed to smile back. "Can we go again?"

19

Valeria and the Bad Boy raced through the small town on his motorbike. Valeria, though not visible through the helmet, was grinning from ear-to-ear as she held on tightly to the Bad Boy's toned chest.

He drove them just outside of town, and Valeria wondered where they were going. He came to a halt in front of a field, and hopped off the motorbike, turning to her. "Come on."

It was five in the morning, and nineteen-year-old Valeria was finding the silence that surrounded them rather eerie. More than anything however, she wondered what was causing the cheeky smile on the Bad Boy's face. "How you feeling?"

"Good," she responded.

"Good."

It had been both one of the most frightening and simultaneously exhilarating moments of Valeria's existence that evening. They had ridden for two hours straight. Yet she was no longer feeling nauseous, and even the trembling had subsided.

"Where are we going?" Valeria asked curiously, as she followed him through the blend of field and forest. All that could be heard were the twigs snapping beneath their feet, and the plants rustling in the wake of their unwanted footsteps.

"It's a surprise," he told her, and her stomach fluttered with butterflies.

What on Earth could it be?

"Come on, I need a clue," Valeria announced, but before he could reply, they suddenly heard a quack.

Yes, a quack.

They turned to one another as they continued walking, and the Bad Boy's eyes were dancing with excitement. It was hard to see what lay ahead in the darkness that surrounded them, but Valeria could just about make out some bushes up ahead.

"Did I just hear...a duck?!" she squealed, but the Bad Boy only smiled at her, and that smile that she had seen a million times over, suddenly looked even more gorgeous in the reflection of the moonlight.

Without saying a word, he took hold of her hand and led them through the bushes. There were a lot of them, and the Bad Boy began to quicken their pace, his power walking quickly turning into jogging, and jogging soon turning into full on sprinting.

It was so dark that they could hardly see where their feet were landing, and Valeria could only pray that she didn't leap feet first into a ditch or trip on a rock.

She had no idea what they were running towards, but she didn't question it. The bushes seemed to go on forever, until finally, they found themselves on the other side of it.

It was then that Valeria saw it in the moonlight – their destination, and what the Bad Boy wanted to show her. A few metres ahead was a lake. Her eyes widened, as she let go of his hand and slowly walked over.

It was a lake the size of a football pitch, with a family of ducks quacking away at each other, and a couple of swans approaching them. They all looked so beautiful in the moonlight that Valeria actually gasped at the sight of them. In all the years she had been coming to this town, she had had no idea that there existed a lake.

Valeria turned to the Bad Boy. "Where exactly are we?!"

"The far end of Lucy's Fields. Outsiders don't know about this lake. It's a town secret. We take turns feeding the ducks and swans."

Valeria couldn't help staring at the Bad Boy with happy eyes, as she took in this new information. "I had...no idea this lake even existed."

The Bad Boy looked chuffed with himself. "First deer, now the secret lake. I may just be opening your eyes to the beauties of this town, Val."

Valeria suddenly had goose bumps hit every inch of her, and she peeled her eyes away from the Bad Boy to take in the beautiful lake. The two swans were now in front of them, staring at them and wondering if they had brought any food.

"I think they like you," the Bad Boy said to her, and she smiled, as she took a deep breath in and spun around slowly, to take in her surroundings, the moment, the beautiful and mesmerising sounds of nature.

She glanced at the ducks swimming together, and the swans staring at them in curiosity.

It was all so perfect, so picturesque, so-

"Can I kiss you?" the Bad Boy whispered, his eyes on her.

Valeria turned to face his curious expression with nothing but complete and utter shock.

20

"I want to go home," nineteen year-old Valeria told the Bad Boy, as the cool breeze sent shivers down her spine and the trees surrounding them rustled in sadness.

It's crazy how in a split second, the atmosphere can completely change. From laughter and excitement, to awkward tension and disappointment. At least for Valeria.

The Bad Boy just asked me if he can kiss me.

He wants me.

He wants me.

He's always wanted me.

Under normal circumstances, this would make Valeria extremely happy. In fact, she would have pounced at him within seconds of learning this information.

However, tonight was no ordinary night, for there was something that Valeria knew, something she hadn't disclosed to the Bad Boy. Something she had discovered only hours earlier.

And things were different now. For he had crossed that line, that barrier. No longer was the lake part of a fairy tale moment, no longer were the swans magical, no longer was this Valeria's favourite evening of the summer so far.

This was now a nightmare.

"Sure," he replied, "let's go."

The journey home on the Bad Boy's motorbike was uncomfortable to say the least. Valeria didn't want to have her arms around his chest but she had to if she wanted to make it home in one piece, and so she held on as lightly as she could.

She was getting angrier with every passing moment, and so she tried her best to forget what he had just asked her.

So timidly, so bluntly, with eyes feigning innocence.

The journey was a blur and she tried to distract herself with other thoughts, like the fact that she was due to go back to the city early tomorrow, and that she didn't need to come back the following summer. Not anymore.

There was nothing to come back for now.

When they arrived outside her house, the Bad Boy parked at the curb and they both hopped off at the same time. She quickly took off her helmet and handed it to him with an expression she desperately hoped gave nothing away.

"Alright, well, thanks," Valeria said, and just as she was about to walk away, the Bad Boy stepped forward.

"I'll walk you to your door."

"No worries, I can manage." She walked off without saying a word.

Come on, you can make it, Val.

Nearly there...

You can do this...

"Are you going to tell me what this is about?" he yelled after her suddenly, but she kept walking. "You're being really immature, you know that? Didn't peg you for the immature type."

Valeria still managed to keep walking.

"I was being a gentleman, you know. Would you have preferred I just lunged at you in the middle of frekin' nowhere?!"

Something snapped inside of Valeria at that last comment, and she turned around.

"Where's Lily tonight?" She walked back over to him. He gulped, his eyes instantly filling with surprise.

"Would *she* think you're a gentleman? For trying to kiss another girl, a girl that wasn't your girlfriend, in the middle of nowhere?"

What the Bad Boy didn't know was that only a few moments before they had met up that night, Valeria had bumped into local bar owner, Geoff, who had mentioned the Bad Boy's girlfriend, Lily.

A girl that Valeria knew nothing about, for the Bad Boy had told her he was single.

As Geoff went on and on about how cute they were together, that they had been cute the entire year they had been together, Valeria suddenly felt very sick.

Yet as she had tried to process this new information, she had spotted the Bad Boy arrive on his motorbike and decided to bury the news, to pretend it didn't exist.

After all, they weren't doing anything wrong.

But now things were different, for he had confirmed to her what he had always wanted from her. He had confirmed to her exactly the type of person he truly was.

A complete and utter disappointment.

"Val-"

"And I'm sure you wouldn't have just wanted a kiss. It's who you are, it's who you've always been. Since that night when you invited me out with Lena. I really should have just cut you off then.

And you know what's funny? You probably did the same thing with Lily, with Lena, and with all the others. The lake, the motorbike rides - it works well, I must say. But it didn't work well enough on me."

There was silence between them, and all that could be heard were the echoes of a dog barking in someone's backyard. "How do you know about Lily?" he asked in a soft tone, as if too afraid to speak with any actual strength.

"This is a small town, Leo. And you two are the town sweethearts. I'd have to be living under a rock not to know."

"Things are not always as they seem, Val. Our relationship, it was great to begin with, but it's gone downhill fast and I'm trying to find a way to get out of it-"

"Please stop. I have no interest in hearing anything about it." Valeria shook her head, forcing a laugh. "This is not even all your fault. I shouldn't have agreed to go out with you tonight, knowing you have Lily.

I shouldn't have agreed to go into the middle of nowhere with you. It was wrong. It was wrong and now it hurts." She looked up at him. "And I have no interest in participating in something that can make me feel this shit about myself." She paused, trying hard to read him, and surprisingly to Valeria, she saw a glimpse of sadness in his eyes. "I'll see you around."

Valeria walked away, her eyes beginning to tear up but she held back with all the strength she could muster.

She got into the house as flashbacks of their adventures over the years rushed over her, and she dove onto the sofa, bursting instantly into tears.

Valeria heard the motorbike roar and take off. She waited.

And waited.

And waited.

Yet the motorbike never returned.

2016

21

Hey I'm here.

As soon as twenty-year old Valeria saw the message, she immediately sprinted through the hustle and bustle of the train station to the platforms.

She had been standing outside the station for a good twenty minutes, trying to understand whether this was a good idea or not. Yet as soon as she saw the text from him, her legs had decided for her.

Valeria trembled as she made her way to the escalators, and she scanned the crowds as she made her way through them, each face that was not his were all quick flickers of disappointment.

Her breathing became heavy, as if every inch of her body was so hungry to see him that if she didn't soon it would self-destruct.

She wanted to see his eyes, his smile, to feel his body touch hers. She wanted to hear his voice, that voice that felt like home to her. The way that only he could make her feel safe, whether they were petting a Rottweiler or running away from the town pervert.

She was a unique version of herself when she was with him, and she couldn't wait to see him. Despite all the bad to him, despite the pain he had caused her over the years. There was an excitement, a thrill, to being reunited with him.

And then all at once, there he was. Valeria saw him in the distance, smiling with those eyes that she knew so well.

Those eyes and smile and face and body that she had only ever seen in his town, on his turf, under his rules.

And now they were in her city, on her turf, and under her rules.

Everything that had happened last summer – all that anger, now seemed juvenile to hold onto. Valeria was a person that could never hold onto anger or hold grudges, even when they were for her own good.

"There she is!" he exclaimed excitedly to the guy with him, and before he could say anything more, Valeria jumped into his arms.

How life is strange, she thought as she hugged the Bad Boy.

Following the events of last summer, Valeria had vowed to not return to the town for at least a few years. In fear of what could happen, or the person she became when she was around him.

Logic seemed to go completely out the window for Valeria in his presence.

And so she had assumed she wouldn't see him for years, she had mentally prepared herself for that scenario. Never had she even thought for a second that he would decide to come to the city to see her the following summer.

Bad Boys don't travel to see other people.

Bad Boys don't make an effort to see other people.

Bad Boys care only for themselves.

He held Valeria tightly, and she could tell he was just as happy to see her as she was to see him. That they both felt sadness towards the fact that they had missed out on last summer together.

But now he was here, to make it up to her.

They let go and she studied him.

Who would have expected it? The tough Bad Boy unable to go another summer without seeing me. To the extent of putting some money to the side, taking time off work, and coming all the way to the city to see me.

"Val! Meet Nick."

Her eyes reluctantly moved from the Bad Boy to a skinny man looking back at her in curiosity.

This was the Bad Boy's 'friend' – in reality Valeria knew that he didn't have any friends he truly trusted, but she had a feeling that to ease the tension and to make sure he behaved, he had brought a work colleague/acquaintance.

"Hi!" All three of them stood awkwardly in the heart of the busy train station, and Valeria clapped her hands together as if attempting to clap away the awkwardness. "Who is ready to see the city?!"

They quickly eased into a comfortable trio, and the next three days were spent showing the boys around the city. Nick was extremely enthusiastic about seeing every corner of the city, whilst the Bad Boy was more interested in talking to Valeria, and learning when she would return to the town.

Her answer was always 'I don't know' every time he asked, and each time the disappointment in his eyes seemed to grow just that little bit more.

The Bad Boy took every chance he got to be alone with Valeria, to ask her how her summer had been, to ask her anything about her life - he wanted to know everything, he wanted to be a part of it. He didn't want any of that to change, and Valeria was secretly grateful for this, though also worried what might happen between them in consequence.

Thankfully, with Nick's extremely boring conversation starters, it left no room for chemistry to resurface between the Bad Boy and Valeria, and by the third day and their last night, she was confident it was gone for good.

There was a fierce storm on their last night in the city, and the three of them ended up in a Chinese restaurant. They had a wonderful dinner, chatting comfortably with their umbrellas drying off under the table.

The Bad Boy and Valeria sat on one side of the table, with Nick opposite them. She was so happy with how their trip had gone that she was even finding herself laughing at Nick's inane jokes.

"Tomorrow back home," Nick suddenly said, and there was silence between them. All that could be heard was the torrential rain hitting hard against the window behind Nick.

Valeria was suddenly and unexpectedly consumed with sadness. The Bad Boy was to go back to his life tomorrow.

Why does this upset me so much?

"Is Lily coming to the airport to pick you up?" Nick asked him, and Valeria gulped. The Bad Boy's girlfriend had cropped up quite a few times in those three days. Each time it had been like a punch to the stomach for Valeria, but she always managed to shake it off.

Besides, they were friends and nothing more.

"No, no. I'll get a taxi."

Despite the pair not even making eye contact, the chemistry between the Bad Boy and herself suddenly hit Valeria, and it hit her hard. So hard that it was difficult not to react. She felt it so abruptly and so aggressively that she was completely taken aback.

Oh shit.

It's back.

It's back.

It's back.

"So I thought maybe if we come back next year, we can go to the carnival, it's a pity we're going to miss it. I mean, we could have delayed our flight..." as Nick rambled on about crap she was not listening to, Valeria took deep breaths in as she tried to understand what was happening.

She imagined kissing the Bad Boy, and cuddling him, and riding him, and having his body on hers. She wanted it all.

She didn't want to just be his friend, despite everything that had happened over the years, and she couldn't understand why.

She wondered if he could feel it too, or if it was all in her head. His eyes were fixed on Nick, as if he were listening intently to him, which made Valeria think that she was alone in this. That it was all one-sided, at least now.

However just as she thought that, the Bad Boy, without taking his eyes off Nick, slowly slid his hand over to Valeria's thigh, and gripped it affectionately.

As if to say, *I feel it too.*

As if to say, *I must touch you, even if only in the subtlest way.*

If this is all I can have, for now.

And there the Bad Boy's hand remained, gripping Valeria's thigh for the remainder of the evening, as they listened to Nick talk, but didn't really hear him at all.

2017

22

When twenty-one-year-old Valeria returned to the small town, she was single. Yet here's the real shocker - when Valeria returned that summer, the Bad Boy was single too. And it was the first time he was single since she had met him.

It took a while for Valeria's mind to process the single version of him, but the more she processed it, the more her desire for him rose to the surface.

After so many years of repressing it, of pushing him away, there was suddenly no need to do so. Not right now. Not whilst he was single and free for the summer.

Since hearing the news two days before travelling, a happy song had started playing in her head. And it continued to play, and play, and play.

She didn't know what had happened with Lily, and she didn't dare ask. Even if deep down Valeria had thought Lily and the Bad Boy would end up getting married. She didn't know why, but she had just always had that feeling.

Valeria and the Bad Boy made plans to see each other her first night back in town, and she couldn't help smiling from ear-to-ear when she saw him standing on her porch with that reckless smile of his.

"Hi." She had flashbacks of them in her city last summer, sitting at that Chinese restaurant with his hand on her leg. Emotions hit her in waves, and she grinned at him.

They were like two excited children on the first day of the summer holidays; they beamed and radiated joy, reflecting each other's mutual mood.

They went to the bar they always went to, the bar that had become theirs. It was the bar that Valeria didn't dare enter with anyone else, in fear that by doing so it would somehow mess with the memories she had with the Bad Boy inside that venue.

As always, the pair spent the entire night catching up on a year's worth of updates, despite the fact that they had text each other constantly for the past twelve months. They playfully argued, told each other stories, and swore at one another. They did all of this with smiles on their faces the entire night; new smiles, smiles that they hadn't ever shared with one another. As if this was a new chapter for them.

Valeria explained to the Bad Boy how much she liked working as an assistant designer. She spoke about how she lived with three other people, two of which she was nearly sure were suffering from depression. She described to the Bad Boy how hard it was to live in the city, and how she believed that the pressure of fast-paced living eventually drowns everyone.

"Not you, though. You like it. You thrive on it, I can tell," the Bad Boy replied. "You were born into it, Val. It's different for you."

And Valeria knew deep down that he was right. The Bad Boy, in turn, had gone on to become a professional mechanic. He specialised, of course, in motorbikes.

There was silence between them once they had described their respective status in life, reminding them once again just how different they really were.

Yet they had never felt closer.

Geoff, the bar owner, threw them out at 3am. They were of course, as always, the last two customers in the bar.

They stumbled out, zig-zagging across the road to his car. Before getting in however, Valeria stood still a moment with the car door open. The Bad Boy looked at her for an explanation, but she said nothing. She slowly smiled, and out of nowhere, Valeria sprinted into the forest in front of them.

It was a spontaneous move, a moment of impulse that had taken over, that had revelled in Valeria's excitement.

She didn't have a plan, she didn't have an ulterior motive – the magic of the forest had simply drawn her in, and she was tired of ignoring it anymore. Of ignoring any of the magic she felt when she was in this town, when she was with the Bad Boy.

She raced away into the blackness of night yelling, 'you'll never catch me!' and giggling to herself like an insane person.

"Val?! Val?!"

She kept running, until she remembered how much she had drunk and a feeling of nausea came over her. Valeria stopped in the middle of the darkness, surrounded completely by forest. She listened intently to her heavy breathing, and a few rustles in the trees.

She kneeled as she tried to catch her breath, embracing the sounds of this beautiful town. Valeria wondered curiously if the Bad Boy had come after her or if he had remained next to his car.

"I'm gonna find you, you know that right? I know this forest much better than you!"

Valeria smiled as soon as she heard his voice, especially as she could feel that he wasn't very far away at all.

She turned around and there he stood, in the distance. They stared at one another for what seemed like an eternity, with a reflection of each other's longing for each other in the other's eyes, their desires finally synching, finally making space for them in the universe.

Valeria was both scared and excited, but more than anything else, she was happy.

Happy for what was about to unfold.

They smiled at one another cunningly, and as if the pair could read each other perfectly, Valeria bolted away from the Bad Boy at the exact same moment the Bad Boy took off after her.

She giggled as she ran, embracing the adrenaline rushing through her veins. Valeria knew he would catch her pretty quickly, and when he did his hands were around her instantly, his strong arms sending goose bumps down her spine.

They spun around a few times drunkenly as Valeria tried to get away, giggling loudly as the Bad Boy grinned. She finally relaxed her back on the tree trunk next to them, the Bad Boy's body unintentionally pushed up against hers.

They laughed, as they looked at one another in what Valeria realised was a terrifying hunger. And then there was silence between them.

A silence that intensified their chemistry.

A silence that spoke of seven years' worth of desire.

A silence that made them both realise that they could no longer deny it to themselves, or to each other.

All at once, their lips crashed into one another's. The chemistry between them hit new levels, exciting levels, as they kissed, as their hands felt each other's bodies as if they were meeting for the first time.

Valeria had a flashback of their entire friendship, as if it was all leading to this very night. From the moment she first saw him at that volleyball tournament, with his innocent eyes and golden, untouched hair, to the motorbike ride where she had clutched his chest so hard he hadn't been able to breathe properly.

It had taken seven years, but they were finally kissing. And they were not innocent, sweet kisses; they were aggressive, lustful kisses, hurried and rough, as if the world could end at any moment. As if they could no longer waste any more time.

Kiss me, Valeria thought, as their tongues collided. *Kiss me for the seven years of wanting this.*

Of craving this.

Of desiring this, with every inch of my soul...

And don't ever stop...

23

Kissing the Bad Boy was, to Valeria, like kissing for the very first time. She had never felt so much passion, so much chemistry, so much adrenaline, from uniting her lips with another person. And it felt so intense, so chemistry-fuelled, so right.

Well sure, they were also groping one another, but that was to be expected after seven years of pining for this exact moment.

They barely came up for air – they just continued to kiss and grope and give into their lust for one another.

That is, until they suddenly heard a rustle in the bushes, and Valeria pulled away from the Bad Boy's lips, exhaling loudly. "What the hell was that?!" she whispered in a panic.

The pair breathed in synch as they looked one another in the darkness of the forest, and the Bad Boy looked at her for a few seconds before responding.

"What was what?" the Bad Boy asked.

But before Valeria could say anything more, they heard the noise again. "That! Don't you hear it?!"

Valeria, though alarmed by the noise she had heard, was also realising as they glanced at one another that they were looking at each other in new ways. That the way they had looked at each other for the past seven years was now gone.

They had crossed lines, and things had now changed forever.

She watched the Bad Boy pull out his knuckle brace.

"Stay here," he said quietly. Valeria continued to watch him as he cautiously took a few steps forward from them, like an overly dedicated bodyguard, and he kept one arm behind him as if to protect Valeria from God knows what.

She smiled as she watched the arm remain firmly in the air, protecting her. And never had she felt safer in her entire life.

Silence ensued and Valeria's fear began to die down, replaced once again with lust, desire and passion.

Impatient now, Valeria pulled him back to her and kissed him authoritatively. He kissed her back just as passionately, and the knuckle brace disappeared under the fallen leaves of the quiet, magical town.

They remained there a while, just kissing, and touching, and giving into their desires for one another. But Valeria didn't let it lead to sex. Not yet.

She wanted to enjoy the chase a bit longer. She wanted that night to be dedicated to their first (and hundredth) kiss. The tortuous exploring of one another's bodies without getting the full experience.

The Bad Boy groaned out in torture at every 'no' Valeria communicated when his hands would try to suggest moving onto sex, but he wouldn't protest any further than a childish groan.

After a couple of hours of making out, Valeria asked the Bad Boy to take her home, and he did so without any complaining.

That night, though they slept in separate beds and houses, neither of them could get to sleep. The rush of the evening had been too much for them to really sleep. There was no time to sleep; the Bad Boy and Valeria had finally kissed, finally admitted to their attraction to one another, after seven years' worth of misunderstandings.

The excitement was far too much to get any sleep.

Yet despite this, the next morning Valeria strolled down the quiet streets of the small town to Pattie's with a spring in her step and a huge smile on her face.

She beamed at the sun, and the sun beamed back at her. She was happy; blissfully happy, as she re-lived the events of the following night over and over again in her head.

She recalled how, as they had kissed, they had sometimes stopped to smile at one another as if they were too shocked to truly understand how it was finally happening. How they had defied every curveball that had been thrown at them. And they continued to make out for two good hours as if each kiss made it that much more real.

Now everything to Valeria – the trees, the mountains, the town, all seemed brighter than usual, more beautiful than usual. Like an alternative universe running on crack cocaine.

When she got to Pattie's, she knocked and Pattie yelled 'come in!'

Valeria pushed open the front door and peeked her head in, as if afraid to enter. Pattie strolled into the foyer drying a plate with the kitchen towel and she smiled at the sight of her.

"Val! Come in, come in!"

Valeria followed her into the kitchen, merrily chirping 'good morning!' only for her jaw to drop. There in Pattie's kitchen stood the Bad Boy, washing the dishes. He grinned at her, and she froze in her tracks.

"Want some breakfast?" asked Pattie.

"Good morning!" The Bad Boy chirped back at her, and she realised she had never seen him so happy. There was a glint in his eyes, a happiness that seemed to directly reflect her own expression, her own eyes. It sent an alarming shiver down her spine.

"Morning, what, uh, what are you doing here?" Valeria asked, still shocked. It was as if she had been thinking about him so much since last night that she had conjured him up in front of her.

"Pattie invited me for breakfast, and now I'm cleaning up," he told her, as if this was all normal behaviour. As if the Bad Boy, who was exactly that – a Bad Boy, usually washed the dishes at other peoples' houses. And just as Valeria tried to take in the image before her, she noticed that he was wearing washing up gloves – bright, yellow washing up gloves. Valeria covered her mouth with her hand to hold back manic laughter.

"Is that...? Are you wearing...? Wow, yes, rightly so – you don't want to ruin your nails, right?" she joked.

The Bad Boy kept his eyes fixed on her as he rinsed the last plate, and slowly pulled the gloves off. Valeria knew this would rattle the Bad Boy. She knew she would pay for this later on, but this is part of why she liked him, why she liked *them*. The way they were able to tease each other so well.

"Oh damn it, we're missing one knife – did I leave it in the garden?" Pattie sighed, getting up and walking out of the house, oblivious to the playful tension between the Bad Boy and Valeria.

Realising she was about to be left alone in the house with the Bad Boy, she scurried after Pattie but the Bad Boy tugged her back by the hand. He twirled her around, and kissed her, passionately.

Valeria let go. "I hope you didn't ruin your nails-"

He instantly put her over his shoulder, and she squealed as he threw them both onto the sofa. Valeria squealed.

"You think you're funny, do you?" he began tickling her, and she continued to squeal, hysterically.

"Don't worry, I know a great nail bar next time you're in the city-"

He jumped up, and pulled off one of Valeria's purple trainers. He then marched outside and she scurried after him.

"Hey! Give me back my shoe!" but he had already thrown it up a tree. It landed on a branch and the Bad Boy seemed satisfied. "I always hated those shoes," he said, turning to Valeria. "See you tonight? I'll pick you up at nine."

She couldn't help but smile as she watched him get into his car. But her smile suddenly disappeared and she limped after him.

"Hey, wait! I need my shoe back! Come back and take it down!"

24

The Bad Boy went to pick Valeria up from her house at precisely 9pm. She stood at the porch, gleaming at the sight of him as he got out of the car. His black Audi purred quietly next to him, and he greeted her with a half-smile.

The pair didn't say much to each other as they got into the car, and Valeria noticed a particular tension in the air between them. The Bad Boy drove them out of town and up the mountains, though she wasn't sure where exactly they were going.

Valeria studied the Bad Boy curiously as he drove without uttering a word, looking straight ahead. There was no small talk, no fighting over the radio; he was mute. All that could be heard was his heavy breathing, and Valeria wasn't sure how to act. She had never seen him like this, and she wondered if he was nervous about where they were going, or more, what they were about to do.

Don't be silly, Valeria.

Bad Boys don't get nervous over sex.

"A bit cold out tonight," she said, trying to make conversation. He eyed the backseat and then Valeria.

"My jacket is at the back if you want it." And it was only then that she realised that he was not wearing his leather jacket, and she wondered why. Especially as it was a particularly cool evening that night. She tried to think back to a time that she had seen him without it and failed.

She didn't dare bring it up, however. Instead she put the jacket on in silence, and didn't breathe another word.

The Bad Boy drove through forests and orchards in complete silence, before eventually came to a halt, and Valeria gasped as she saw the beautiful viewpoint in front of her. She jumped out of the car, and leapt towards what she quickly came to realise was the edge of a cliff.

"Hey, careful," the Bad Boy said, as he followed her out of the car and marched over. She stopped a few metres from the edge and looked out at all the lights.

"That one over there is our town," he told her, pointing to a scatter of lights to the left.

Our town, Valeria thought to herself.

I guess this town is mine too.

After all these years...

He leaned in to kiss her and they began to make out. Yet the new tension between them was still there, still nagging away at Valeria, and she began to feel agitated. Something was wrong, but she didn't know what it was.

He wasn't kissing her the way he had kissed her the previous night. Something had shifted. Something had changed. And she didn't know how to find out what it was. Valeria suddenly let go, and ran into the forest. When she turned around to give him a cheeky smile, the Bad Boy gave her a confused look.

"Come on, let's go explore this forest! It's beautiful!"

The Bad Boy followed her, but his confused look remained. "Yes, and it's also really cold up here."

"Do you want your jacket back?" Valeria began to take it off, but he shook his head and helped her put it back on. They began walking into the black of night and she realised that they always seemed to be making their way into darkness.

Twigs snapped under their feet and she understood that running into the forest had not helped – if anything the tension was rising even more now with every passing second.

She could feel the chemistry between the Bad Boy and herself dying, slipping through her fingers, and she couldn't let it happen. Not after how long it had taken to reach this point.

Valeria suddenly turned around and jumped him, grabbing his face with both her hands as she kissed him, passionately.

Taken aback, it took him a few seconds to react and kiss Valeria back. But when he did, his kisses were just as aggressive as hers, and they were both immediately struck by the passion.

Yes, it's back. It's back! Valeria thought to herself.

It's back and here to stay!

As they continued to kiss and touch and grab, they walked back towards the car, and he kissed Valeria zealously as he pushed her up against the car door.

When he let go of her lips, she thought it was to open the door. She imagined him looking at her with his broody Bad Boy eyes, before sexily opening the car door and pulling her inside.

She imagined him pulling both their clothes off, grabbing a condom, and going for it. That it would finally be happening, it would finally be taking place. The way it should have happened years ago. Or maybe this was the way it was always supposed to happen.

But that's not what Valeria saw happen when she looked at him. The Bad Boy didn't open the car door, nor take their clothes off, nor look for a condom. When Valeria looked at him, she only saw turmoil in his eyes.

Turmoil she did not understand, or know how to comprehend. Yet as soon as she saw it, she connected with it so viciously that she felt something sharp hit her right in the stomach.

"I can't do this," he suddenly said. "Val, I can't."

Valeria kept her eyes fixed on his, afraid to hear the answer but knowing she had to ask.

"What's going on?"

Her 'What's going on?' came out so soft, and so very afraid of what she was going to hear come out of his mouth, as if on some level, the universe had already told her.

"Lily's pregnant."

25

All in a nanosecond, it was like Valeria's entire world came crashing down around her, and she knew straight away, that that one sentence from the Bad Boy changed absolutely everything.

Every possible scenario she had ever dreamed up in her head with the Bad Boy disappeared, evaporated into thin air, in only a nanosecond.

"She's pregnant, and it's mine. It's mine, Val!" his voice now no longer seemed like that of a tough, loner Bad Boy, but that of a wimpy and needy teenage boy. A lost and scared teenage boy, not sure what to do or how to become a man, but knowing that he had to somehow.

There was only one door now.

Valeria felt immediately sick, but she knew she had to ask. She knew deep down the answer, it was gnawing away at her, and she had to know, before she would run away from this person in front of her, this coward that she would soon no longer be able to look in the eye anymore.

"How many months?" she asked firmly, as if she wasn't about to burst into tears or start screaming at the Bad Boy for every pain he had caused her in the last seven years.

Valeria watched as the Bad Boy gulped and looked away in shame, opening the passenger car door for her, but she immediately slammed it shut.

"How many months, Leo?" she yelled. "How many months?! Can you answer?! How many fucking months?"

"E-eight months. She's eight months pregnant."

Valeria's voice box vanished into oblivion as she took in his words. As disgust filled every inch of her body. Her head began spinning in a mixture of sadness, guilt and revolt.

"She's due next month. We broke up six months ago, she said she was going to have an abortion but she didn't. She told me soon after, and we patched things up.

I've known, I've known this whole time since you got into town, and I've tried to forget it, I've tried to pretend I'm not becoming a father, but I am. I am, Val!"

Valeria thought about all the messages they had sent to each other in the past eight months. She imagined a pregnant and vulnerable Lily crying in her bed, wondering where the father of her baby is.

Why he couldn't be loyal to her.

Why he had never been able to be loyal to her.

She imagined her beautiful, sad face, at being the girlfriend of the Bad Boy, and the mother of his child.

It was in this moment that Valeria saw the Bad Boy for who he truly was – a lying, conniving coward who thought he was tough and cool, but really he was nothing short of an avoider of real life.

She re-lived his flirting and teasing, hoping secretly to kiss her, to have sex with her, whilst out there was a woman carrying his baby.

The Bad Boy looked at Valeria for a reaction, but her head was spinning so fast now that she could hardly move, let alone speak. Remembering his kisses just a few seconds ago, she kneeled over in the bushes and began spitting out his saliva.

His saliva that was now mixed with hers. She couldn't tell which was his and which was hers, but she didn't care. She needed every bit of him to disappear from her life.

Forever.

Never to return.

Never to gain her trust like this again.

Never to be fooled by his charm, by his Bad Boy ways.

And so she continued spitting, and spitting, as he breathed heavily next to her in the darkness that overlooked a town she could no longer claim to be her happy place.

For the only words running through her head on loop were:

This is all your fault for trusting a Bad Boy.

This is all your fault for trusting a Bad Boy.

This is all your fault for trusting a Bad Boy.

This is all your fault for trusting a Bad Boy.

This is all your fault for trusting a Bad Boy.

This is all your fault for trusting a Bad Boy.

This is all your fault for trusting a Bad Boy.

This is all your fault for trusting a Bad Boy.

This is all your fault for trusting a Bad Boy.

This is all your fault for trusting a Bad Boy.

This is all your fault for trusting a Bad Boy.

This is all your fault for trusting a Bad Boy.

This is all your fault for trusting a Bad Boy.

This is all your fault for trusting a Bad Boy.

This is all your fault for trusting a Bad Boy.

26

When Valeria was done spitting out as much of the Bad Boy's saliva as she could, she walked back to the car and got in. She didn't make eye contact with the Bad Boy, nor did she say anything.

There was nothing she wanted less than to be back in his car, to have him drive her home, but she had no other choice. She was in the middle of nowhere, and calling Pattie to come get her would mean explaining why she was up a mountain at 10pm with a guy who was about to become the father of someone else's child.

In small towns, gossip ruins you. And she didn't want gossip to ruin her to the point that she could never return. No, it was better to let him drive her home, and then never see him again. She loved this town too much to give it up for a douchebag.

She saw from the corner of her eye the Bad Boy walk around the car and get in the driver's seat. Valeria kept her eyes fixed ahead and gritted her teeth.

She was angry – furious in fact. But she knew shouting at him would be futile. He was simply evil, and nothing could ever change that.

The Bad Boy started the engine, and as he reversed out of there, Valeria kept her eyes fixed on the view of the small town as it became smaller and smaller, until it was no longer visible to her.

The Bad Boy drove in silence, switching off the radio within seconds. Valeria remembered every happy moment shared between them, and she knew they were now all tainted, all poisoned by the reality of the situation. By the realisation that the boy sitting next to her was after nothing but sex. No matter what time of day. This was who he was. This was who he would always be.

Every smile.

Every drink he had ever bought her.

Every text he had ever sent her.

Every touch.

Every motorbike ride.

It now held no value whatsoever, because each and every single thing he had ever done for her had had an ulterior motive. He didn't like her or care for her; she was just a challenge.

A challenge she would never allow him to win. Ever.

It took Valeria a few seconds to realise they had arrived outside her house and that the Bad Boy had stopped the car. Snapping back to reality, she quickly took off her seatbelt, and got out.

She slammed the door shut without making eye contact with the Bad Boy, and as she did so she realised she was now trembling. Valeria didn't know how long she had been trembling for, but she was, profusely, and she didn't know how to stop.

As she crossed the road over to her house, she hoped and hoped that she wouldn't hear the driver's door click open. When it did, with her back to the car, she closed her eyes in disappointment.

"Val!" the Bad Boy called, urgently, and she had never heard urgency in his tone before. Some people on the street looked on to see what the yelling was about, but Valeria didn't acknowledge it. She didn't turn around, nor reply; she just kept walking.

"Val!" he yelled again, even more urgency in his voice this time.

Bad Boys are never desperate, Valeria thought to herself, but she shook it off. She had seven years' worth of a habit forgiving him and believing his words.

Not anymore.

"Val!" he yelled again, yet she only kept walking. Arriving at her front door, she quickly got out her keys and, trembling still, managed to open the door.

As soon as she was in the house, she slammed the door behind her and locked it.

Valeria let out a sigh, but it was not of relief. It was of guilt, and terror, and sadness, and anger.

She pulled out her phone quickly, knowing exactly what she needed to do.

Valeria found the Bad Boy's number and clicked 'block this person', just as she heard him start the engine and drive off.

She stared at his profile picture on her phone a long while; he was now a person that could no longer contact her, or be a part of her life in any way, shape, or form.

And as she stared at the screen, she collapsed on a chair next to her, bursting into tears. Loud, painful, embarrassed tears. Mourning the death of a a fantasy she had carried with her for an entire seven years.

2018

27

"Oh my God Val, you have to try this pineapple cocktail!" Ben said, as he appeared on the terrace with a bright smile.

Valeria, whose eyes were locked with the incredible view down below, pulled her gaze away from the magic and turned around to welcome Ben back to the terrace with a gracious smile.

"Pineapple?! I love pineapple flavoured cocktails!"

Gleeful with pride for choosing the right drink for Valeria, he handed her a glass as he took a sip from his.

"Where did the guys get to?" Valeria asked him, and he looked around the inside of the bar through the open double doors. House music blasted from the speakers placed in either corner of the spacious balcony. It was a pretty packed evening, but then again it was Friday night and Valeria was used to being here most weeknights too, when it was far less hectic.

"Mmm, I think Michael went to the bathroom and Georgia is getting chatted up by the doorman."

Valeria rolled her eyes and took a sip from her drink. As she did so, she couldn't help but study Ben as he approached and looked out at the view, as if he had never seen it before. As if he hadn't grown up in the same small town that she was fascinated with. A town that, somewhere in this view, held its place.

It was hard to believe that the Ben before her now was the same Ben she had met at age fourteen, one week before meeting the Bad Boy. It was even harder to believe that it was the same Ben she had bumped into again at age sixteen, when Valeria had been out with the Bad Boy and Lena.

He had turned into such a man now – manly facial hair, a hardened face, and wise eyes. He looked much older than his twenty-five years, and he was fascinating company to Valeria.

He was, after all, the crush that had never really been.

Valeria turned around to face the view too, and they stood with their arms just inches apart on the railing.

"So...had a good summer?" he asked, and Valeria detected an element of hope in his voice. The hope that he had been able to look after this summer, that she had had a good time in his presence.

"I did. A lot. It's been really fun."

You would have expected Valeria to not avoid the small town like the plague after what had happened with the Bad Boy and his shocking revelation the previous summer.

Yet, though that might have been something Valeria would have done at seventeen, or even twenty, it was no longer her methodology in life at age twenty-two.

Though extremely embarrassed and ashamed for her weak decisions, she had decided to come back for the summer again. She had, after all, run away back to the city the previous summer after the Bad Boy's confession.

She had come back for her 22nd birthday however, and remained for the entire summer. That, turned out to be for three whole months; the longest time she had ever stayed there, even when she was a student. She had quit her job and decided to take the summer for herself.

She gave zero fucks about bumping into the Bad Boy. This was her town too, and she would do whatever she pleased with her life.

It was now a full year since Valeria had blocked the Bad Boy on all apps, and nothing had changed between them in that time. They had had no contact whatsoever.

On her first night back three months earlier, Valeria had attended a party in the next town with Pattie, and that's where she had bumped into Ben. They had clicked straight away, became instantly friends, and introduced her to his group of friends.

They were a quirky bunch – the type to go out most nights, have a few beers and then go home and watch a series like Friends. They weren't the types of people to go out and get hammered, or ride motorbikes really fast or get into fights at bars.

Valeria found it refreshing to go out and not worry about getting into any sort of trouble. It made her feel comfortable, and relaxed with her surroundings. She couldn't remember the last time she had felt this way in the last eight summers.

"Good," Ben said, and they turned to face one another at the same moment. Valeria watched as Ben's eyes dropped from her face, to her chest, to her legs. She was wearing a sleek and sexy green dress that highlighted her perky boobs and tanned legs. She didn't usually dress like this, but it was Friday night and she had had an intense desire to dress up for it.

Valeria knew that the way Ben was looking at her was not platonic, that he hoped for something more, yet she also knew that he wouldn't make a move. He was too hesitant, too reserved with his romantic tendencies, to take their friendship to the next level, and Valeria was happy with this, for she knew she couldn't handle anything other than platonic with anyone in the countryside anymore.

Incredibly, in the three months that Valeria had lived in the small town, she had not seen the Bad Boy once. Rumour had it he had moved in with Lily and her parents, who lived in a small town a half an hour drive away.

Rumour then had it that Lily had had the baby at the end of the previous summer; a girl, and they named her Annabelle. It hit Valeria like a punch to the stomach, and she imagined little Annabelle sleeping in her mother's stomach as she had kissed her father on top of a mountain.

She remembered just how much she had wanted to have sex with Annabelle's father, whilst she was sleeping in her mother's stomach.

It made her sick to the stomach whenever she thought about it, and so she tried her best not to ever think about it.

"Guys, I got a date with the doorman!" Georgia yelled, as she strolled onto the terrace. It broke the spell between Ben and Valeria, as Ben turned to grin at Georgia.

"The skinny one or the chubby one?" he asked her, yet Valeria turned her back to them to look out at the view.

As she took in the beautiful scenery and the clusters of small towns she saw before her, she couldn't help wonder which of these towns held the Bad Boy. Because despite all the bad, despite all the pain, despite all the daggers to the heart, Valeria still missed him, and she couldn't understand why.

Why his presence still remained, *even after everything*.

28

Twenty-two-year-old Valeria semi-walked and semi-danced through the streets of the small town, as she listened to some club music. She was not paying attention to the beautiful skies, the gorgeous scenery, or the fresh air.

After all, she had been living in the small town for the entire summer – three whole months. She was used to how gorgeous her surroundings were.

Valeria got out her phone to see a message from Ben; a kiss emoji. She smiled and sent a kiss emoji back. Putting her phone away, she went back to dancing through the streets at three in the afternoon as she made her way to Pattie's.

However, just as she went crazy to the chorus of the club classic blasting through her headphones, she felt a car tailing her.

She immediately turned to take a peek from the corner of her eye, and could see a jeep driving a couple of metres behind her. Valeria looked down – she was still walking on the pavement, so she couldn't understand what this person's problem was.

Maybe it's a crazy psycho killer.

Okay stay calm, Val.

Just keep walking.

She did this for a few more seconds, before remembering that she was in the most innocent, small town to ever exist. It had to be someone she knew.

She turned around and squinted at the driver's seat. Her eyes widened at who she saw behind the wheel, and she froze, slowly pulling her headphones down around her neck. The car stopped next to her, and the Bad Boy scrolled down the window. It was the first time she was seeing him since that dreadful night on the top of that mountain an entire year ago.

And now looking at him, it felt as if it had all happened a decade ago.

"Hey," he said. Looking into his unhappy eyes, and studying his tired face, every inch of his skin looked exhausted. Not only that, but he didn't seem Valeria's age anymore. He seemed at least five years older since the last time they had seen one another.

No one would ever guess he was only twenty-three, and the more she studied him, the more she realised she no longer recognised the person in front of her. To think that she had once kissed those lips seemed absolutely insane to her now.

It had been a long, fulfilling and healing year for Valeria. Even if she did still miss him.

"Hey," she replied, and they looked at each other a good while before either of them said anything more. In fact, they were only broken by their spell when they heard a noise.

A baby crying, to be precise.

Valeria eyed the backseat to see a very cute one-year old girl crying.

Annabelle.

Guilt struck Valeria as soon as her eyes met the baby's, a guilt she had never felt before.

A guilt so strong that it was hard not to react.

A guilt so aggressive that she was suddenly finding it hard to stand.

Flashbacks of them up on that damn mountain, in that damn forest, in that damn darkness, re-emerged. After she had neatly stacked away those memories at the back of her mind, there they were again, as clear as day.

They flooded her mind and she had no way to stop them, to prevent them from taking over. And as she re-lived them kissing, she imagined an eight-month pregnant Lily with this girl in her tummy, waiting to meet her parents.

All whilst his father was kissing another girl, a complete *bitch*, in some forest.

Flashbacks of the intensity of their kisses pushed their way into Valeria's mind and took over every inch of her.

Moments that she had, at the time, deemed authentic, timeless, infinite, now drowned in a guilt so tremendously strong that she was hit almost instantly with a profound nausea.

A nausea that couldn't allow her to remain standing there.

"She's very cute," Valeria told him, and she meant it. But before he could reply, she blurted out 'see you around' and marched off down the street.

She begged and begged herself to hear the sound of him driving away, wishing and hoping that he didn't follow her.

She secretly sighed in relief as she heard the Bad Boy turn the car around and *vroom* off in the opposite direction.

Valeria turned a corner and took a few deep breaths in. An old woman eyed her from across the road, but it was okay – it was their secret.

For she was the only one who could ever know that *Valeria still cared.*

29

When Valeria stepped out onto the balcony of the club to get some fresh air, she knew she was bored. It was her last week in the small town, after nearly four months there.

A lot had changed since the start of the summer – Valeria now worked in the local bar to make some extra pocket money, and she was an unofficial member of Ben's social group. All of this prompted Valeria to spend her summer getting herself into far less trouble than normal.

She was healthy. She was healed. Yet she was constantly and undoubtedly incredibly bored.

She had had fun, sure, but something was missing, and she knew it. She just didn't know how to fix it.

The feeling of perpetual boredom gnawed away at her every second of the day and she knew she had to figure out what exactly it was, but she kept putting it off, telling herself she would figure it out tomorrow. That she was simply not ready yet. But perhaps, deep inside, she was putting off finding the answer for she did not want to face what the answer could be, and what it could mean.

Or even, what type of person it could make her.

"Val!" yelled Ben, as the balcony doors flew open, the sound of loud house music thumping from inside the club and invading Valeria's ears. "I bought you a Long Island iced tea!"

This was now Valeria's favourite drink, as of the last three weeks. She took a sip as she looked out solemnly at the view.

It appeared that not even a new favourite alcoholic drink could make Valeria feel complete.

She thanked Ben as he lit up a cigarette next to her. The balcony doors closed, and they were left with a much quieter ambience.

"It's beautiful out here," Valeria said, looking out at the incredible view of the mountains.

Ben took a few moments before he replied. "You know Val, this is your last week here. You should live it up. Drown your sorrows in alcohol, in the countryside, in your friends."

Valeria thought about Ben's words a moment as he blew out smoke rings, and a smile slowly appeared across her face.

She looked down at her drink in curiosity, and to Ben's surprise, she suddenly took a huge gulp.

Half the drink disappeared.

Ben laughed and *woo*'d, patting Valeria on the back. "Welcome to the dark side!"

She glugged down the rest of her drink and felt the alcohol burning and oozing inside of her. She felt alive, and happy, and, anything but bored.

As she looked into Ben's green-blue eyes, it was as if she only just realised how attractive he really was.

His dirty blonde hair, his silver earring in his right ear, and his chiselled jaw that made Valeria weak at the knees. It was incredible how she hadn't noticed his sex appeal the entire summer, when in front of her now stood a ferociously attractive young man.

She continued to stare at him as her libido began to wake up, and he gulped, as he blew out another smoke ring, noticing her intense stare.

Fuck this, she suddenly thought, and so she grabbed his face with both her hands and kissed him.

She kissed him with passion, and desire, and curiosity.

She kissed him to find answers, to find meaning from her summer spent in the small town.

She kissed him to make that evening different from every single evening of the past four months.

Though thrown off, Ben kissed her back just as passionately, and just as eager, if not more, and he held her face with his free hand as they continued to kiss.

Valeria was in control, the way she had imagined she would be if she ever kissed Ben. She was dominant, and powerful, and she owned this game. It made her feel good. As if she couldn't believe she had spent the entire summer not doing this.

She suddenly let go, and they smiled at one another.

"Well, uh, that was unexpected," Ben said, and he was about to continue when Valeria wrapped her arms around his neck and kissed him some more. He placed his hands around her waist as they went at a slightly calmer pace.

Valeria was in charge.

She was a queen.

She was an independent, strong female who went after what she wanted.

Valeria had in fact, come a long way since the days of being a timid teenager. No longer was she a quiet teenager, shying away from making the first move or speaking her mind.

Valeria was finally herself, comfortable in her own skin, and a strong young woman successfully battling a fast-paced and complex world.

She was in control, and nobody would ever be able to take that control away.

Ben's smile was even wider when they let go a second time, as if he was liking kissing Valeria more and more with every passing second.

"Well, that was a bit overdue," Valeria told him, nonchalantly.

"Uh, well," Ben cleared his throat as he tried to recover. "I, uh, I definitely agree. I've wanted to kiss you all summer."

Valeria's heart began racing at the excitement of kissing Ben, of having someone look at her with admiration the way Ben currently was, after a long summer of abstinence.

He glanced at her empty glass and nodded at it. "Shall we go get another?"

"Sure," she said, as they made their way back into the club.

Valeria felt on top of the world, like nothing could ever disrupt her feeling of power and control; she felt indestructible.

As they walked across the dance floor, Ben's hand around Valeria's waist and and the pair of them smiling like small children receiving an endless amount of chocolate, they bumped into someone.

It was a girl clearly not looking where she was going, and her drink spilled all over Valeria's red dress.

"Oh, I'm so sorry!" she squealed, and Valeria looked up from the spill on her dress to the girl standing in front of her.

She was beautiful; gorgeous emerald eyes that shone in the lights of the club and firey red hair. Her big red lips matched her hair colour and she was wearing a similar red dress.

"It's okay-" Valeria began, but as her eyes moved from the girl to the guy with her, Valeria suddenly lost her voice box.

Before her stood the Bad Boy, with his hand on the girl's waist. The Bad Boy noticed her at the exact same time Valeria noticed him, and they locked eyes as if in a trance.

Gone was Valeria's strength, and feeling of control. In fact, in only a matter of seconds, Valeria had never felt less in control. Her voice box now obsolete, she didn't know how to react.

What the hell is he doing here?

Isn't he supposed to be at home, being a father?

Doesn't he live with Lily?

I've never met Lily but I've seen her around, I know what she looks like and this is definitely not her!

Valeria noticed that the Bad Boy was not wearing his leather jacket, and it felt as if it wasn't him standing before her but some sort of doppelganger. Valeria's vulnerability surfaced within nanoseconds, the void in her stomach from most of the past year returning and reminding Valeria that it had never left.

"Seriously, I'm so sorry-" the female stranger rambled on, but neither one of them were listening to her. They just kept staring at one another in shock, and curiosity, and sadness, and anger.

The Bad Boy looked from Ben, to Valeria, to Ben again. He couldn't quite believe what he was seeing, as if he was jealous of who was with Valeria, of who had the honour of taking her out, of having his arm around her waist.

Valeria found the pain of looking into the Bad Boy's eyes and only re-living what had happened up on that mountain the previous summer all too much for her. She marched across the dance floor in an instant, without even saying so much as a 'goodbye'.

The Bad Boy didn't move nor react, and perhaps this, more than anything, was what hurt Valeria the most.

30

Valeria bounced around on the dance floor of the club as Tinie Tempah blasted from the speakers. She was grinning from ear-to-ear, really concentrating on her supposed dance moves. She was almost grimacing as she moved, and if you were to ask her what she was doing, she would say she was 'making the most of every moment'.

There were people on the dance floor watching her as she danced, but she didn't notice. She didn't notice because Valeria was completely and utterly intoxicated. She could hardly see – in fact, she could hardly stand.

This was indeed by far the most drunk Valeria had ever been in her entire life.

"Val-" Ben's voice boomed over the music, a hand gently touching her elbow, but she ignored it. "Val - don't you think you've had enough?!" His voice lacked confidence, as if he wasn't really too sure what to do.

He could see the hurt in her eyes, he understood that by seeing the Bad Boy it had triggered something in her. He knew nothing about their history, but he knew that there had existed something between them. And he also knew that by the way she had reacted to seeing him that there was still something there. This made it hard for him to focus on how drunk she was when inside his chest, his heart was slowly breaking.

Valeria continued to ignore him.

"Val, I'm serious, people are watching you-"

"So what?! Let them watch! Maybe they want to learn a dance move or two!" Valeria blurted out, as she went back to dancing by herself.

She knew she was hurting Ben, she knew it, and yet she couldn't stop herself from being a complete and utter bitch to him.

She felt Ben place another hand on her arm, this time the grip a little tighter, and that little bit more authoritative. His lips leaned in and stopped in front of her right ear.

"You're making a gigantic ass of yourself," he yelled over the music, and even though Valeria was so intoxicated she saw two Bens in front of her, she understood instantly what his problem was.

She studied him (or more, both of them) for a few seconds before responding. "Too embarrassed to be seen with me?" she laughed drunkenly to herself. "You can fuck off then."

Ben gulped, and shook his head in disappointment before storming off the dance floor. "Find your own ride home then!" he yelled as he disappeared, but Valeria didn't care. She didn't care that she had hurt Ben, that she had likely ruined their friendship/budding romance. She just wanted to dance, and drink, and be happy. To drown out the pain.

The rest didn't matter.

Valeria's eyes glossed over the crowd to find someone, anyone, from Ben's friendship group, but she quickly realised that none of them were there anymore.

When did they all leave?

She didn't panic, however.

I mean, the club is only a mile from my house. No big deal.

Yet the club suddenly felt claustrophobic, and memories she had tried so damn hard to forget were starting to resurface, along with the feelings attached to them. And with them resurfaced pain she had tried to bottle up for an entire year. They were spiralling out of her with no way to stop it.

She decided that she needed to get out of this club as fast as humanly possible. She needed her house, her bed, her pillow.

That, she said to herself, *would solve everything.*

A male stranger dancing near Valeria asked her if she needed a ride home.

"I'll be fine, thanks," she replied, without even looking at him.

Plus, surely it's safer for me to walk than for some random guy to give me a lift?

It was still summer in the small town but it got cold in the mountains at night. Valeria shivered as she hugged her red dress, wishing she wasn't in the countryside, wishing she was in the city, where she could call a taxi. Where she had friends who didn't abandon her at clubs.

It was dark out, really dark. In fact, it was so dark that Valeria had to get out her phone torch to guide the way.

She began walking the main road; it was a steep road and a downhill journey, with no barriers on the side of the road. In fact, if a car (or even Valeria in this case) were to swerve off course, they would fall down a very steep forest.

Despite being incredibly drunk, Valeria was aware of this, but decided not to think about it. After all, she had no other choice.

She debated going back, but quickly remembered she had no one to take her home anymore. Ben had left her here to fend for herself, and that was exactly what she would do.

She began to tremble, though she was not sure if it was from fear or the cold or even both. She knew this road well during the day, but at night it was a completely different experience.

"Hey lady, it's dangerous out here," said a deep voice, and now Valeria's heart was racing. She knew she couldn't run – she was far too intoxicated to do that, and there was a huge chance she would fall straight into the forest beneath her.

No, she knew she only had one option. She turned around.

A man in his forties with food in his beard and a certain vulgarity in his eyes, slowly approached. He was a few metres behind her, and despite meeting nearly all the locals during the summer, Valeria had no idea who the man in front of her was.

"I asked you if you wanted a ride home, you declined," he said, grinning at Valeria to show her his missing teeth.

Suddenly Valeria didn't feel drunk anymore. All she felt was fear. Complete and utter fear for her own life.

She didn't want to die like this. She didn't want this to be the way her life ended.

"I'm good to walk, thanks," Valeria said with the biggest smile she could muster, and she turned around to be on her way.

"Hey wait," he called, and Valeria froze, her back to the stranger, as she closed her eyes in hearing his protest. She knew this man wouldn't go away now.

She was trapped, with absolutely no idea how she could escape.

"Why don't you turn your pretty little head around for me darling, so I can see you?" the man said, and Valeria took a tremendously fearful and deep breath in, as she slowly turned around...

31

"These roads are dangerous you know," the stranger said to Valeria, as his eyes analysed every inch of her physical appearance from head to toe. Valeria couldn't look him in the eye and instead looked out at the road, praying for a car to pass. But none did.

Life seemed to be like that sometimes – just when you needed another human to be around, you found yourself completely and utterly stranded. with way too many Long Island iced teas running through your blood.

"A pretty girl like you, you'd probably cause cars to go off the roads," the stranger continued, and Valeria could feel his smile growing wider, showing more of his non-existent teeth.

"I'd better be going, I'm late to meet my boyfriend," Valeria said, as she tried, for the third time, to walk away. She walked fast and with determination, hoping and praying that he didn't follow her.

"Your boyfriend left you in that club alone. He's not coming back anytime soon," the stranger said, and Valeria could hear his footsteps behind her.

He was, indeed, following her.

Valeria took deep breaths in, wishing she had a bottle of water with her so she could try to sober up, but she didn't, and she could see that she was not walking in a straight line. All it would take for her to drop down to her death in the forest was a few footsteps in the wrong direction. There was no way she could run away from this stranger. The only thing she could do was continue to walk, carefully, ahead.

"Hey, where you going?" the man said. "The road is long sweetheart, and I got all night."

"Leave me alone!" Valeria suddenly yelled. "I already called the police." She was lying through her teeth though; her phone was in her bag and she was terrified to get it out and dial, afraid that the vulgar stranger would grab it off her and throw it into the forest beneath them.

"Wait for me," he ordered, and Valeria ignored his request, trying to quicken her pace, but she could feel him getting nearer and nearer. "I said, wait for me!"

She felt his vile hands grab her arms and she screamed, loudly, for him to let her go. She screamed and screamed, pushing him away but he continued to bounce back. He was horrendously strong, especially against Valeria's vulnerable, drunk self.

He kept pulling her to him, trying to kiss her, but she continued to push him away at every attempt. With every try came a scream from Valeria; louder and more desperate than the last.

And as she continued to battle the evil in front of her, she suddenly heard the sound of a motorbike engine.

"Help!" she yelled, looking out at the road she came from but seeing nothing. "Help!" she bellowed again, and then she saw it. The motorbike. The man on the motorbike. He wasn't wearing a helmet, but Valeria had already known it would be the Bad Boy.

Somehow, she had known. And she had never been more grateful to see him in their entire seven years of knowing each other.

He raced towards them, and before the engine had completely come to a halt, he jumped off and started punching the stranger.

Two punches, three punches, four punches...

The man was clearly unconscious but the Bad Boy kept going. Valeria, now sobbing, tugged at the hems of his t-shirt.

"Leo, leave it. Leo. Leave it! He's out. He's out!"

The Bad Boy slowly stopped, and spat on the man's face, the saliva running down his chin.

Valeria tried to pull the Bad Boy away from the stranger's limp body, but he wouldn't budge. He kept watching him in disgust; the saliva dripping down onto the stranger's jacket and the Bad Boy eyes remain fixated.

"Leave it, Leo. Leave it. Let's just go. We have to go." Valeria said, as tears continued to stream down her face.

But just as the Bad Boy continued to stare at the stranger, the stranger suddenly rose and grabbed him by his t-shirt, head butting him.

Valeria screamed as the Bad Boy bounced back, groaning in pain. She watched them as they fought, only steps away from their death into the forest that waited below. Valeria tried to intervene; punching the stranger in the stomach, but the Bad Boy pushed her back and told her to stay away.

She obeyed, and as the pair continued their tug-of-war on each other's bodies, the Bad Boy was able to get in a punch, and another, and the stranger toppled backwards, yelling in desperation for them to save his life, as he fell instantly into the forest beneath them, plummeting feet first into his death.

The Bad Boy and Valeria leapt forward to try and save him, but it was too late. They could only be witnesses to the body as it flew through the air, and down into the darkness. A thump was eventually heard, and the desperate pleas for a life to be saved suddenly stopped.

And all that remained was silence.

32

An eerie and shocked silence surrounded the Bad Boy and Valeria, as they stood at the edge of the road, leaning over the forest and looking down into the blackness that lay beneath them.

Some rustles could be heard in the trees from night animals, but that was it.

Valeria could hear the Bad Boy breathing just as loudly as she was as he stood beside her, his eyes fixated on the forest.

She re-lived the vulgar man's scared eyes as he had plummeted to what they could only assume was his death.

They had killed someone. Accidentally, sure, but they had killed someone. They had witnessed someone lose their life.

Valeria had never even seen a particularly bloody fight happen before her, and now she had witnessed a death. Right in front of her eyes.

One moment he was here, the next he was gone.

One moment he was breathing, the next he wasn't.

One moment he had his vile hands on her, the next the Bad Boy was breaking his nose.

Though the pair of them didn't say anything for at least a solid minute, Valeria suddenly found herself resurfacing back into reality. Back into a life where her voice box and her logical thinking played a major part in her actions.

"We-we-we-we killed him," she managed to say. "We fucking killed him-"

"We don't know that!" the Bad Boy suddenly said, turning to her as if he too, was emerging back into reality.

"Was he bionic or something?! That jump is huge, nobody could survive that!" Valeria yelled, and she had no idea why she was yelling.

"Val, we don't know what happened to him!" the Bad Boy yelled back, and just as Valeria was about to reply, to argue with him, they heard a car engine and saw a small green Peugeot race past them. They remained mute, turning their backs to the car and instead looking out at the forest again.

As soon as it was out of sight, Valeria immediately turned to the Bad Boy. "We have to call the police! We have to tell them what happened, how it wasn't our fault, how we-"

"I know, I know," the Bad Boy got out his phone, and groaned in annoyance. "Signal here is shit, damn mountains. Let's go back to the bar-"

"Wait, let me check mine," Valeria got out her phone and saw four bars on her screen. "Signal's fine for me, let me call-"

"No, let's go back to the bar and do it," the Bad Boy told her calmly, but Valeria only gave him a puzzled look as he walked back to his motorbike.

"Why?"

"It's just better, Val. Maybe one of his friends will follow him out here to check up on him; let's go back to a public space."

Valeria thought about it and decided the Bad Boy was probably right. She knew that she would feel a lot better in a public space too.

She hopped on at the back of his motorbike, and the engine purred into life.

Valeria held on tightly to the Bad Boy, even though it was strange to do so without his leather jacket on. She felt nauseous but tried to keep all her Long Island iced teas at bay. At least until they would stop.

As they rode down the road, Valeria kept re-living the vulgar stranger's hands on her arms; how rough and cold they had felt against her skin.

She remembered her pleads for him to let her go, of how trapped she had felt, of how much she had hated him for thinking he could do whatever he wanted with another human being.

And then she remembered his fall into death. The look of sadness, and repentance in his eyes as he fell. And somehow it was this image that repeated itself in her head the most. The fact that ten minutes ago that vulgar man was alive, and now he was not.

And it was irreversible.

Valeria was thankful that the Bad Boy was driving slowly, but it was an entire minute or two into the journey that she realised he was going in the completely wrong direction.

In fact, he was going in the direction of her house.

He's running away from the scene of the crime! Valeria realised, and she began pulling at his t-shirt, shouting for him to stop, to turn back, to not be an asshole, a coward, a putrid human being, but he didn't even turn around or acknowledge her protests.

Instead, he only accelerated and it became harder and harder for Valeria to protest, in fear she may make him crash them into a tree.

They arrived outside Valeria's house and she hopped off the bike before it had even fully come to a halt.

"What the hell, Leo?! You can't just run away from a crime scene! I refuse to do that, I refuse to allow you to run away-"

"I'm not running away, Val. You are," the Bad Boy said, matter-of-factly.

Valeria gave him a confused look. "Come again?"

"I'm going back, and I'm going to call the police. I'm going to give them a statement, and I'm going to take it from there."

"I'm coming with you! We-"

"There is no '*we*', Val. You're due back in the city in less than a week, and you're about to start a new job, or at least that's what Pattie told me. You're going to be a junior designer, right? It's exactly what you've been waiting for. You really want to put your life on hold for that waste of space? In and out of trial for manslaughter or self defence or whatever this ends up being?"

Valeria could not believe what she was hearing. The Bad Boy wanted to protect her, she saw it in his eyes. The way he had always wanted to protect her. Even when it meant making himself more culpable for a crime he didn't mean to commit. Even if it meant risking himself being put in prison.

They stared at one another for what seemed like a lifetime; his eyes were full of his undefeatable duty to protect her, and hers were full of intrigue.

She suddenly had a flashback of the first time she had ever gone out with the Bad Boy at age sixteen. She had been sitting in the passenger seat of his car, Lena at the back, and she had watched him as he told Lena he needed to make sure Valeria went home in one piece. He had the same look of dutiful responsibility towards her wellbeing that he had now.

So many things had changed over the years, but one thing had always remained the same: The Bad Boy's need to protect her.

"Leo, there were two of us up there, and the only two who know what happened-"

"I was the one that was fighting him, Val. Not you. I can win this. And I will."

Valeria knew she couldn't fight him on this, he wouldn't let her. Yet the sequence of events that night was leaving her head spinning.

She had spent the past year hating the Bad Boy's guts and planning to never speak to him again. And yet now, now everything was different. Everything from their past was forgiven. It was forgotten. The person currently standing in front of her was someone who had always loved her, who had always wanted her to be happy.

There was nothing else that mattered in the world.

"Leave tomorrow, take the first train out. No one will connect you to the crime." He told her, but Valeria shook her head and forced a laugh.

"This is ridiculous, I-"

But it was too late. The engine suddenly *vroomed* into gear and the Bad Boy was gone within seconds, leaving only a cloud of gravel dust in his trail.

2019

November

33

Twenty-three-year-old Valeria walked out of the train station semi-excited and semi-anxious, pulling her huge luggage bag behind her. The icy cold wind hit her face and she pulled her scarf up to her nose.

It was her first time returning to the countryside in winter since childhood. It was weird for Valeria to be back here in a season that wasn't summer, but the snow soon relaxed her. It made everything look even more beautiful than it did in summer.

She looked around at the people she passed, looking for someone in particular in the faces that she saw.

"Val!" yelled a male voice, and she turned around with a big grin on her face, only to spot a stranger calling out to another woman, a woman who was also presumably called Val.

Valeria sighed, yet her smile remained as she began to walk across the car park of the train station.

It was good to be back. It was wonderful, actually. She had never felt better. She had a good job back in the city, a good life, and good people around her.

Her scarf however, was up to her nose not only to hide her from the cold, but to hide her from the residents of the small town.

You see, this wasn't the train station for the small town. This was the train station a few stops from the small town.

Valeria wasn't heading in that direction. Not yet. She was expected back in the small town only in a couple of days, only after the weekend. In fact, no one even knew she was back in the countryside except for one person.

Valeria spotted a black Audi parked in the far end of the car park and nervously approached, squinting at the man sitting in the driver's seat. He looked pensive in thought, as he stared straight ahead.

It was only when Valeria was a metre away from the car that he spotted her and smiled.

Suddenly flashbacks of their times shared together over the years came rushing back to her, and she couldn't help but smile.

The Bad Boy scrolled down the window. "Hey."

"Hey," Valeria replied, and they found it hard to look each other in the eye for more than a nanosecond. She scurried over to the boot, threw her luggage in, and got in at the passenger's side. His expression seemed to mirror hers – a mix of anxiety and excitement in their eyes in the realisation that their friendship tomorrow will have changed forever.

"Ready?" he asked her. She nodded and they looked away from one another as the engine roared into life, and off they drove.

Surprisingly for both of them, an awkwardness hit them like a tornado, and it was immediately unbearable. They put on the radio, they small talked about her train ride, but none of it seemed to help matters. They knew why it was awkward. They knew that they had not seen each other since that fateful night, a whole year and three months earlier. The night that Leonard Raymond had died. The night that neither of them dared to bring up.

The night that they simply wanted to forget.

Valeria had obeyed the Bad Boy's request that night and packed up her stuff, taking the first train back to the city the next morning.

A few hours after her return to the city, Valeria heard through Pattie that the Bad Boy had been arrested for manslaughter. He was released on bail, and in and out of court over the next year or so.

Fortunately, the Bad Boy had had an excellent lawyer, and in the same month of Valeria's twenty third birthday, the case was dismissed, and the Bad Boy relieved of all charges.

It was something that nobody had seen coming. After all, the Bad Boy was already a criminal in his own name. Everyone had expected him to end up in prison.

And yet, it hadn't happened.

When Pattie told Valeria the verdict, a tremendous sense of relief had washed over her.

Having hardly spoken in a year, she had decided to text the Bad Boy to congratulate him. The Bad Boy had had an entire trial to deal with, not to mention a family to look after. Valeria had not wanted to disturb him.

But when she heard the news of his trial, she knew everything was over, and she had the courage to reach out, to reunite.

The Bad Boy thanked her, and they began to converse as if they had never spent time apart. As if nothing had ever come between their friendship, ever.

As if, on some level, they had been present for one another for every second of everyday for the past nine years.

Friendly texts in the first few weeks quickly turned flirtatious, and the Bad Boy told Valeria how he had moved out of Lily's parents' home the previous summer and now lived back at home with his dad.

He was single. For real, this time. And so was Valeria.

Somewhere along their flirtatious texting, they had come up with a plan to spend a weekend alone together at the Bad Boy's cabin up in the mountains. Away from the small town, away from prying eyes, and away from their lives back home.

And thus it became painfully obvious to the both of them that the awkward silence they were sharing in that car was not only caused by the fact that they hadn't seen each other since that fateful night more than a year ago, but also by the knowledge that they were driving towards everything they had ever wanted from one another.

Not only that, but that they were finally going to get it.

Valeria realised that their awkwardness needed to be demolished in one way or another if this were to actually happen however, and so she reached out and put on the radio. She switched station, as if their problem was the choice of music. A cheesy eighties track blasted, and so she switched station again, only to hear Madonna. It didn't seem like a Madonna-appropriate moment, and so she kept going, each station worse than the last.

"Are you done yet?!" blurted out the Bad Boy, playfully irritated.

"No!"

"Geez, you're so annoying!"

"Oh? Me? Annoying? Excuse me!" Valeria continued to switch stations, at a quicker pace now just to aggravate him. The Bad Boy's grin only grew bigger as he shook his head at her, reminding her of just how much she desired him, how much she had pined for him over the years.

Just how much she found him attractive.

She remembered their first kiss, she remembered the way they had touched each other's bodies, she remembered his lips on every inch of her skin...

"Stop!" the Bad Boy yelled, as he tried to pull her hand away from the radio.

There it was, that touch.

That chemistry.

That electricity.

Valeria tried her best to play it cool, though she knew particular parts of her body were starting to wake up.

She swatted his hand away.

"Hey! Stop! I'm driving!"

Valeria stopped on a religious radio station, with a nun talking about the importance of family. She raised an eyebrow at the Bad Boy, and lay back in her seat, coolly.

"Seriously?"

"Yes. I missed today's sermon," she told him, in a playfully tone. The Bad Boy slowly reached out to change the radio station and she again swatted his hand away.

"Oh my God, you are a *child*!" he preached, and Valeria giggled. They had both relaxed, and suddenly neither of them were anxious, only excited for what lay ahead.

Of what they had been waiting for for an entire nine years. Ever since that moment they had locked eyes at that volleyball tournament that warm summers' night.

34

Valeria and the Bad Boy were glad to be back in the warm car. Armed with fast takeaway boxes, they sighed in relief. The Bad Boy placed his on Valeria's lap and started the engine.

Valeria's entire body was shivering from the cold, despite the gloves, scarf, hat and winter coat. She had forgotten how cold the countryside got in winter.

"Wait, aren't you going to eat it first?!" Valeria told him, as he swerved round a corner and she clutched both takeaway boxes tightly.

"Nope, we're still an hour and a half away from the cabin; we need to get out there before it starts snowing again," the Bad Boy told her.

"And why exactly did you buy food then if by the time you're able to eat it it will be cold?"

"Well, it's this amazing concept Val called multi tasking!" One of his hands suddenly left the steering wheel to reach out to the box, open it up, grab his burger and take a huge bite out of it. Valeria looked on in dismay.

"Yum!" he yelled, with a mouthful of burger.

He was doing it by purpose - multi tasking like that. He was waiting for Valeria to cringe her nose up in disgust the way she always did when he did something disgusting. He hadn't seen this look in years and seeing it again in that moment only made him smile back at her.

He couldn't explain it, but her cringed up nose gave him more joy than anything else in his entire life, across the entire nine years, including every girlfriend he had ever had, but excluding the moment his daughter had been born and every moment he had shared with her since.

He stared at her as he ate and she nudged his shoulder.

"Keep your eyes on the road you animal, or we'll end up in a ditch instead of your cabin!"

He obeyed, and a sudden silence encompassed them, as the idea of falling into a ditch reminded them both simultaneously of the same thing.

You see, the pair may have diluted any awkwardness between them now, but that didn't mean they had for one second forgotten Leonard Raymond, or his sad eyes, or his body falling to its death right before their eyes.

They had to be careful, however. If they let visions of Leonard Raymond's sad eyes haunt them it would kill them and they knew it. Which is why over the past year and three months, the pair of them had both found ways to remember the evil in Leonard Raymond.

To remember that the entire night's events had happened in nothing but self defence. That evil didn't live in either of them, and that it never would.

The moment passed, just like everything else, and the pair were back. The Bad Boy took another bite from his burger and purposely began biting very loudly. Valeria giggled and pushed his arm, nearly causing the Bad Boy to drop mayonnaise onto his lap.

"Hey! I'm driving!" he told her, playfully annoyed.

"Then eat properly!"

"Then don't push me when I'm driving!"

Valeria, of course, pushed him again, simply to disobey his orders. He looked at her with his warm smile. Her heart (and vagina) were ready to explode, she could feel it.

To show him just how much she felt their connection, their bond. After all these years.

"Hey! Don't!" he continued to protest, and Valeria continued to do the opposite just to annoy him.

She liked seeing him get playfully annoyed, and she liked touching him; his arm, his chest, his face. Her pushes only seemed to bring them closer together.

In more ways than one.

35

When Valeria opened the car door and stepped outside, the cold air hit every inch of her face and made her instantly shiver. She stepped out with her scarf up to her nose, and looked up at the mountain house in front of them.

Valeria knew they were very high up, even if she couldn't see anything. Next to the house was only darkness, and what felt like oblivion.

"Come on," the Bad Boy said, leading the way to the side of the house where there were wooden steps filled with snow.

Thank goodness I wore my winter boots for this trip, Valeria thought as she followed the Bad Boy up the steps.

That wasn't the only thought on Valeria's mind, however. With every step that she took, she knew that they were a step closer to being alone.

In a house.

Together.

Something that they hadn't experienced in years. In fact, not since Valeria's eighteenth birthday.

The Bad Boy suddenly stopped at the top step, and pulled out a bunch of keys from his leather jacket. Valeria heard the key turn and the door open, revealing a foyer that the Bad Boy stepped into. She watched him as he wiped his boots on the welcome mat. He signalled for her to do the same and she followed.

"I'll go get our stuff," the Bad Boy announced, leaving Valeria alone in the house. She took off her shoes in the awkward manner that is only present when you are in someone else's house for the first time, and slowly made her way across the foyer into the kitchen.

It was a simple place, with only the essentials, and it was clear that no one lived here on a full time basis. It was simply a weekend getaway, a nice place in the mountains when you wanted to escape life.

"I'll go switch the electricity on," the Bad Boy said, once he had brought their luggage in. Valeria simply nodded at him, and took off her coat, knowing the moment was coming.

The moment where they would be alone in a house, in the mountains.

After all these years of waiting and hoping for this moment, here it was. Right in front of them.

When the Bad Boy returned, Valeria was looking at a polaroid picture of the Bad Boy with who she assumed was his uncle. She recognised his face – she had seen him around town on plenty of occasions. They sometimes said hi to one another, and he seemed pleasant enough.

"Want something to eat?" the Bad Boy asked, pulling out a packet of pasta from his backpack.

Valeria laughed, nervously. There was something about being alone in a house with the Bad Boy, in the middle of nowhere, that made Valeria incredibly nervous and shy. As if she reverted back to fourteen year-old her; the very innocent and naive young girl who had stood before the Bad Boy at that volleyball tournament all those years ago.

She had a flashback of that volleyball hitting her leg, and the moment she had laid eyes on him for the very first time.

It made her smile.

"You brought pasta?" she asked him.

He cocked up an eyebrow at her. "Yeah, why? Did you want us to starve?"

Valeria shook her head. "No, I just...I just didn't envision you thinking ahead."

The Bad Boy forced a nervous laugh, and he too, felt like a foolish teenager all over again. He remembered seeing Valeria walking off that volleyball court that warm summers' night an entire decade ago and it sent shivers down his spine. Not that he would let Valeria see that, of course.

He smiled, coolly. "I also bought tomato sauce. Did *you* think ahead?"

"Uh, no, I guess I didn't-" Valeria stuttered, only getting more nervous and awkward by the second.

"Well then it's good I did! Can you boil some water? There's a pan in the top cupboard."

Valeria was on her feet in a nanosecond. The awkwardness between them was only getting worse, and so the Bad Boy casually put on some music to accompany them. As they cooked, and listened to 90s punk rock, they appeared to relax.

The intolerable tension between them seemed to disappear and they returned to being Valeria and the Bad Boy; two people who cared deeply for one another and who had done so for nine whole years.

They laughed and they joked, shoving each other playfully as they cooked, and bopping their heads to the music.

They told each other stories from the past year; stories that captured each other's attention so much that they over cooked their pasta and were left with soggy penne for dinner.

This didn't seem to phase them in the slightest; in fact, they couldn't seem to stop laughing over it, to the point that it made Valeria's stomach ache.

She hadn't laughed that hard in years; that sort of laughter that had you gasping for air. And this was before they had even started in on the beer the Bad Boy had brought.

They ate with animated expressions as they continued to share stories, as if they had last seen each other yesterday. As if the negative events that they had experienced in the last nine years had never happened. Only the good moments, the happy times, the situations that had created and maintained their bond, all of these years.

The moments that had shown each other just how much they cared.

It was late into the night when there was silence at the dinner table; they were out of stories, out of conversation, and out of songs. The last song on the Bad Boy's playlist had just finished, and suddenly, the house was quiet. Deathly quiet.

The awkwardness, the nerves, it all came rushing back to both of them. They knew what was coming next. And they could no longer delay it.

"Shall we go upstairs to sleep then?" the Bad Boy asked, and Valeria nodded. They cleaned the kitchen in awkward silence and headed up. The stairs were wooden and creaky, only adding to the tension that now suffocated both of them.

Valeria's heart raced as she followed the Bad Boy up the stairs, and as they walked into the bedroom, she saw the two beds - the king size, and the single.

"I'll take this one," the Bad Boy said, as he nodded at the single bed, and Valeria gawped, trying to process his words. She had assumed that he would be sleeping in the king size with her. She had assumed they were going to have wild, passionate sex and not sleep all night. She had assumed that he wanted her, that he craved her, the same way she craved him.

Had she been wrong? Had she read too much into their flirtatious texts?

Nothing seemed to make sense.

The Bad Boy raised an eyebrow at her with a cheeky grin. "What, you didn't think we were sharing a bed, did you?"

Well, we did just spent the past four weeks flirting with one another and fantasising about this very moment...

Was it really that insane of me to make that assumption?

Valeria shook off her thoughts. "No, of course not - this bed is mine," she said, and she dumped her stuff on the king sized bed, announcing that she was going to go brush her teeth.

36

As Valeria lay in bed, pretending to watch television, she couldn't quite believe the situation she had found herself in. After all the flirting and teasing that the Bad Boy and herself had done via texting over the past few weeks, after the nine years' worth of chemistry and the incredible bond that they had created with each other in this time, and it was all going to lead to nothing.

Nothing.

The last thing Valeria had expected when she had agreed to come out to his uncle's mountain house was to be sitting on different beds, watching some crappy reality show.

It's Saturday night, for goodness sake. And I did not give up my weekend like this to hang out in separate beds with the Bad Boy like a couple of virgins.

Valeria wondered if she had made a mistake, if she had misunderstood his intentions, if he had really intended to come out here to watch some crappy reality show with her all long.

Yet these thoughts didn't last long. Soon enough Valeria pushed those ideas away and remembered that she knew the Bad Boy, that she knew him *really* well. She knew that he liked to tease, to see a person's reaction.

To test a person's reaction.

He liked to pretend that he didn't want you, to see your reaction. Just like all those years ago in front of that lake. The Bad Boy's 'Can I kiss you?' had sprung up out of nowhere, with no previous clues that he wanted her, that he desired her.

Right now in his uncle's mountain house it was the same exact thing, she was sure of it. All she needed to do was play along.

That or, well, jump him.

The Bad Boy had not moved from his single bed since they had arrived upstairs, and his eyes remained glued to the television. She inwardly sighed, remembering adventures they had shared together, racing through the countryside.

Who could have predicted that the first time the Bad Boy and Valeria would be alone together in a house in the mountains, far away from everyone, they would spend it in separate beds, watching a reality show?

On a Saturday night!

Valeria turned her head to get a view of the Bad Boy again, but as she did so it took all of her self control to stop herself from gasping. He was standing next to her bed.

She watched him slowly as he casually climbed onto the king size and parked himself next to her.

"What are you doing?" she asked him.

"I thought we could watch this show together," he told her, nonchalantly. She didn't reply. The best thing she could do was not reply at all, to play it cool, to not show that she wanted to pounce at him with every ounce of her sexual being.

And so there they sat, next to each other, watching some trashy reality show like an old married couple. With their backs against the cold wall, their arms were touching, and Valeria wanted so desperately to kiss him, to ride him, to be doing all of that already.

But she didn't want to make the first move. Somehow the tension, the waiting, the torture, was a pleasure in itself.

After all, they had been doing it for the most part of nine years. They were experts.

The Bad Boy suddenly lay down on his side, facing her. Valeria kept her eyes fixed on the damn show as if she didn't even notice, but from the corner of her eye, she slowly saw a hand reach out and poke her on the hip.

She squealed quietly and batted his hand away. He did it again, and again, until eventually she gave in, and poked him back.

As soon as Valeria did this, he instantly pulled her down onto the bed with him, beginning to tickle her as she tried pathetically to playfully push him away, giggling.

"Stop!" she said, in fits of laughter.

"Stop what? I'm not doing anything!" he replied, with that smile that lit up his face only when he was with Valeria. It was a smile that only showed itself in her presence.

Their playful fighting soon tired out, and the pair somehow ended up cuddling underneath the covers; her head on his chest, as they lay sideways on the bed.

Valeria loved how his skin felt against hers, how his arms felt around her, with his breath on her neck.

How long she had waited for this, fantasised about this, and it was finally happening.

He began softly kissing her neck, nearing closer and closer to her mouth.

Peck. Peck. Peck.

Each soft kiss sent butterflies to her stomach, and awoke every inch of her body.

Peck.

Peck.

Peck.

Each kiss became more and more urgent however, accelerating in frequency, as he neared closer and closer to her lips.

Just as he reached her chin and made his way up, Valeria tilted her head, and they both leaned in to kiss, delicately.

They kissed so slowly and so softly that it was as if what they were sharing was so fragile that they didn't want to break it. As if they both knew exactly where this was leading, and how this night would change the course of their relationship forever.

Valeria had flashbacks of their friendship over the years, from every small touch that had made her crave him endlessly, to how safe she had always felt being on the back of his motorcycle. He was the only Bad Boy in her life, and he was finally hers for the taking.

Their kisses however couldn't remain sweet and innocent for long, and as they quickly turned wildly passionate, clothes started coming off and tongues rolling across each other's bodies.

Valeria realised she had never wanted someone more.

It's finally happening...

The Bad Boy and I...together...

They were suddenly fully naked, incredibly horny for one another, and there was only one thing missing. The Bad Boy hopped off the bed, grabbed a condom from his backpack, and raced back to Valeria. He climbed on top of her with a smile and began to kiss her as he slowly entered her.

That's strange, Valeria thought to herself. *Out of all the times I have imagined having sex with the Bad Boy, I never imagined it happening in missionary, of all positions...*

But Valeria didn't care. She just wanted to be with him, finally. To have him. To experience sex with him.

Yet just as he began to thrust, something strange happened. Something Valeria could never have predicted.

As he began to thrust, she began to notice a shift. A change in chemistry. It was instant, and it was painful, and before Valeria knew what hit her, she knew that deep inside her, something had just changed. Something made her feel incredibly different.

Suddenly the Bad Boy's kisses weren't sexy. Suddenly his body wasn't something she craved or desired. Suddenly his pumping away at her wasn't everything she had ever wanted.

It was the opposite.

She no longer liked his skin touching hers, she no longer wanted him to be naked, nor on top of him or in her.

She instantly froze, terrified and confused as to what was happening. After all the years of lusting for one another, and it had evaporated into thin air as soon as they had stripped. As soon as the possibility of the pair having sex was no longer a pipe dream. As soon as he had started pumping away inside of her.

She didn't understand it, she couldn't understand it, but she was sure of one thing in that moment – she didn't want to have sex with the Bad Boy.

37

Valeria cringed as the Bad Boy kissed her neck. She tried her damn hardest to get back the chemistry, to align her nine-year fantasy of this moment with reality, but the more she tried, the more she cringed.

Get a hold of yourself, Valeria!

Take control.

She pushed him off her, and climbed on top. She began kissing him as she rode him, but nothing about this moment felt right. Never had she desired anyone less than she did the Bad Boy in this moment.

She tried to ride him with at least a fraction of the skills she had developed over the years, but her lack of desire resulted in a lack of energy. She tried to moan and fake her enthusiasm as she rode him too, but it came out forced and awkward. The fact that she now shared zero desire for him meant that sex was now also painful for Valeria.

Yet she tried and tried to rectify the moment, to find her desire for him again, to make it passionate and wild. But she was failing and she slowly stopped, wishing she was far away, wishing she had chosen to return to the small town instead, wishing she had never text him at all. Because now, now she had to deal with a confused Bad Boy on her hands.

"Are you a virgin?" he calmly asked, softly. "It's okay if you are..."

The idea that at twenty-three Valeria was a virgin was so laughable that she imagined herself watching this moment like a scene in a film at cinema, along with every man she had slept with until then, and all of them laughing so hard they fell off their chairs.

She remembered every sexual encounter she had had up until then and it made her want to burst into a fit of giggles right then and there, in front of the Bad Boy. But she knew she couldn't do that.

She was acting nervous, awkward, and tense. She was acting as if she were afraid of his body, his lips, his kisses. When in reality, what Valeria was afraid of was where his kisses would or could lead. Not because sex scared her, but because sex was simply something she did not want with the Bad Boy. Not anymore. And Valeria was starting to realise that maybe, she never had.

"What?! No! We're not teens anymore, I have countless exes! Too many if we're honest!"

Naturally, the more Valeria tried to defend the fact that she wasn't a virgin, the more she sounded like one. She opened her mouth to explain, yet as she did so, she studied his curious eyes. Eyes that had always looked out for her, always put her well being first, and she realised it was most certainly better that he thought that she was a virgin than know the truth. The last thing in the world she wanted him to uncover was that after nine years of craving each other, she didn't want to sleep with him.

At all.

As Valeria looked into his eyes, she saw their entire path up to this moment.

The volleyball tournament at fourteen years old, the first time they were in a car alone together as teenagers, standing outside her house with his motorbike on her eighteenth birthday, punching the town psycho for her, and the adrenaline rush the first time she got onto the back of his motorbike.

They had shared so much together, and in some ways they had even grown up together. How could she hurt him like that? After all this time...

Valeria prepared her sweeter, more innocent tone. "I guess it's jus, I uh, I don't have sex very often. The truth is, sex is a big deal for me."

Valeria knew that her fantasy with the Bad Boy was slowly beginning to die in front of her, and that there was nothing she could do to stop it.

The Bad Boy rubbed her arms affectionately. "Hey, it's okay, we can take it slow."

Right, slow. Or maybe not at all?

Before Valeria could say anything in response, the Bad Boy was slowly kissing her and climbing on top of her again. She wanted to suggest they try again in the morning, to give it a rest, but she didn't want to disappoint him, or their nine-year fantasy. She saw fourteen year-old her tapping her Vans shoes in irritation, screaming at her for not enjoying sex with the Bad Boy, after everything!

She realised it probably had nothing to do with her desire for him and way more to do with the fact that they had planned this. Planned sex never goes as planned. Planned sex never matches the reality.

Knowing this, Valeria decided she could fix this. She could push past the plan of sex and into actually enjoying it.

With all the energy she could muster, Valeria shut out all her negative thoughts, closed her eyes, and took in his kisses. She tried to think of times she had craved him so desperately, of past kisses and desires.

And at first, it worked. She enjoyed it. Well, a fraction of it. Yes, it was fun. Pleasurable.

But after a minute or so, the pleasure factor faded, as her thoughts started to shift to weird places.

Like that strange guy at school who touched stale chewing gum stuck under the classroom tables.

And that ginger bloke with a pervy smile who asked for her number at a club one night a few years ago.

And Jack, the guy she had briefly dated before it turned out he had baths with his adult cousin.

And just like that, it all became clear to Valeria.

The way I feel about the Bad Boy is the the same way I feel about those weird guys.

It made her skin crawl the same way. He was, to Valeria, in the same box as them, for reasons she could not explain.

Holy shit, Valeria thought to herself. *I have absolutely no desire for the Bad Boy at all.*

She instantly opened her eyes. *"Stop!"*

38

Valeria took deep breaths in the darkness of the bedroom as she sat up, and she realised she was trembling.

"Hey, what's going on?" the Bad Boy asked, just inches from her face. He brushed her fringe away from her face with his fingers as he studied her.

"Nothing, I just need to pee. I can't have sex like this; I need to pee first."

And just like any couple having sex for the first time, hearing the word 'pee' seemed to put (an even further) damper on their sexual chemistry.

The Bad Boy nodded and Valeria leapt out of bed. She slipped on her underwear, as if the Bad Boy was not allowed to see her body naked unless they were having sex, and vanished out of the room.

She hopped down the creaky stairs and to the bathroom, putting down the seat and burying her head in her hands.

Valeria was mortified. She had never yelled 'stop!' during sex in her entire twenty-three in existence.

She had never stripped naked and had the guy start having sex with her for her to realise she no longer wanted him.

This had never happened to her, and she would never have guessed that if it ever were to happen, it would be with the Bad Boy.

She wanted to cry, she wanted to scream, but she was too frustrated to do either. Valeria didn't understand what was going on, and it suddenly dawned on her just how far away from society they currently were. They were in the middle of nowhere, and stuck there the entire night.

She splashed her face with cold water, dried herself off, and hopped back up the stairs. The Bad Boy was pretending to watch the reality show and hiding his bruised ego. Valeria walked over to the bed with sexy determination, grabbing him by the back of the neck and kissing him passionately.

Taken aback, the Bad Boy took a few seconds to react but was suddenly kissing her back with as much passion. She pushed him on his back, thinking of all the times she had wanted him, desired him, craved him.

The chemistry was suddenly coursing through her veins, giving her that adrenaline that Valeria knew so well. She moaned in his mouth, which only made him even hornier, but he was not daring to initiate anything now. He was waiting for Valeria to control everything.

Maybe this is going to work.
Maybe this is going to work.
Maybe this is going to work.

She kept kissing him, and moaning, running her fingers all over his body, until there was nothing more to do but...

She felt immense desire for him, for how tough and manly and protective he was of her. Of how he had punched someone for her, and taken the entire murder trial on by himself, how him travelling to the city just to see her. For how he had always treated women like shit, but not her. She was special. He loved her.

Like really, truly *loved* her.

They had a special relationship. It was irreplaceable. It was the type you'd find in books. That people loved to hear about and invest in and root for.

Relieved that she was able to re-capture the chemistry, she gained even more confidence and began to ride him with enthusiasm. The Bad Boy smiled at the view, as if it was a view he had waited nine years to see.

A hand appeared on Valeria's face as she rode him, and she gave him the best she had. He began to moan too, and they moaned in synch, as she continued to ride him.

This went on for a few more moments, until she could no longer fight it.

She could not keep it out anymore.

And in one fleeting moment, her desire for the Bad Boy vanished, and she knew that that was it.

There was nothing else she could do. She had tried, and tried, and tried.

Disappointed and disillusioned with herself, she rose slowly, and collapsed next to him.
The Bad Boy caressed her cheek but she was too embarrassed to even look at him.

"Lie down," he whispered to her. Still in a daze, Valeria obeyed and lay to her side. The Bad Boy's arm became her blanket, his face in her hair, his hot breath on her neck.

And this, to Valeria, was by far the best and worst moment of the entire evening. The Bad Boy switched off the television and the bedside lamp.

There was suddenly darkness, and Valeria had never felt more relieved.

39

When twenty-three year-old Valeria awoke the next morning, it took a few seconds for her to remember and re-live the events of the previous night.

The Bad Boy picking her up at the train station, driving them up to his uncle's cabin in the woods, and the nine-year-old chemistry between them dying a quick and very painful death right in front of them. At least for Valeria.

She hadn't been able to fall asleep until 6AM. It was now 7:48AM and she was already awake again.

It appeared that despite their nine-year friendship, Valeria was not comfortable enough with the Bad Boy to fall asleep next to him. She also kept trying to understand why he was suddenly not attractive to her. Why her sexual desires of an entire decade no longer existed. Why she was now repelled by the thought of having sex with him.

Despite spending most of the night trying to work it out, at 7:51AM that Saturday morning, she still didn't have any answers.

Plus, it didn't help that the Bad Boy decided to spoon her for half the night; his body was like an unwanted hot water bottle, involuntarily transferring his body heat to her. She had felt like a boiling vegetable for most of the night. She hadn't had the balls to pull away from him or tell him to his face that she was too hot to be spooned like a married couple. I mean, she was already not having sex with him after teasing him for nine years about it. She didn't need to add more salt to the wound.

The fun however hadn't really started until the Bad Boy had fallen asleep and begun snoring in her ear. Valeria had wished desperately to be somewhere else, anywhere else, and wondered how she had got herself into such a web of weird.

It seemed like an entire eternity had passed when, at 7:59AM, she felt the Bad Boy move next to her. He was on his side of the bed now, scrunched up in a ball in the corner with his back to her.

He yawned and turned around to face Valeria. She tried to read his eyes but saw nothing.

Is he angry about last night, or did it not phase him? Or worst of all, does he know I don't find him attractive anymore?

"Morning," Valeria croaked. As she watched the Bad Boy slowly start to wake up, she realised that this was the first time she had ever woken up next to the Bad Boy. In all the scenarios she had ever fantasised about this moment in the past nine years, none of them had involved a night quite like the one she had just experienced.

"Morning," the Bad Boy responded in a neutral tone.

Valeria wasn't sure what to expect and so she waited, and watched, curious as to what he'd do next. He kissed her, and she felt nothing.

Absolutely nothing.

No rush of excitement.

No lust.

Nothing.

They let go and he studied her face. She prayed that he wasn't somehow tapping into her lack of attraction towards him – the last thing Valeria wanted to do was hurt him, for him to see just how empty she felt inside when he kissed her.

He suddenly pounced at her, kissing her with passion, but she couldn't stand it. She didn't want it. She couldn't.

She let go very quickly. Too quickly. As if she had already made her decision. As if she had made her decision the night before, or even worse, nine whole years ago. She just hadn't realised it until then.

Valeria tried to read him, but nothing. He remained unphased by her reaction and instead yawned. She watched him as he sat up and checked his phone for a few minutes. She decided to do the same.

And so there they sat, their backs against the wall as they checked their phones in silence. It was an incredibly awkward feeling and Valeria opened her mouth to say something, anything, yet she couldn't think of anything to say. She decided instead to focus back on her phone.

A few minutes passed, the awkwardness and sadness continuing to build. The more time that passed, the more tension built between them.

How on Earth are we going to get through the rest of the weekend together?

The Bad Boy suddenly turned to Valeria. "So I think I'm gonna go pick up my daughter early. Lily says she'd like to go to the salon at lunch."

Relief came over to Valeria at the blindly obvious revelation that he wanted to leave ASAP too.

Of course he bloody does Val, you're both not having the greatest time on Earth.

"Okay." They exchanged forced smiles, and she watched him get out of bed to put on his jeans. There was a weird mixture of relief and happiness to soon be out of the cabin and away from it all.

As she showered, he tidied up the room, put off the fireplace downstairs, and cleaned up the kitchen. Valeria wanted to help but it seemed he wanted to be left to it. And so after her shower, she pretended she had lots of stuff to pack up when in reality she hadn't unpacked anything to begin with.

She floated in and out from the bathroom to the kitchen, until she eventually decided to go back upstairs to see how he was doing in the bedroom. He had been there a while.

When Valeria entered, the Bad Boy was making the bed. "Oh, need some help?" she said, walking over.

"No, I got it. Don't worry." Though his words were not unkind, his tone carried no emotion. As if Valeria were a stranger. As if she were a cashier in a store trying to sell him something.

She backed away, deciding to be evasive rather than confront the situation. Plus, she wasn't sure what she'd say if she did decide to confront this new-found tension. After all, she was having a hard enough time deciphering the reasons behind it herself.

She stood awkwardly in the bedroom when she suddenly froze as she noticed the view outside the window. It was incredible. They were completely surrounded by mountains, and fog. They were really high up.

She slowly walked over to the window as if in a daze. It was the view she had yet to see. The view whose presence she had felt when they had stepped out of the car and walked the pathway to the front door.

Oh how things had been different just twelve hours ago.

She gasped as she took in the gorgeous view and lost herself in the colours. Dawn had always reminded her of new beginnings. Her smile slowly began to leave her, as it suddenly struck her that her friendship with the Bad Boy, once they would walk out of here, would never be the same again.

"Come on, let's go. We're set." The Bad Boy said, and she gulped, trying to bat away the sadness now encompassing her. She hadn't had enough time to take in the beauty of the view and yet, she knew she had to go. There was no other choice.

Valeria grabbed her stuff, forced an 'okay' and followed the Bad Boy out.

40

Valeria drummed her fingers on the window as the tension between her and the Bad Boy only grew in the silence of his black Audi. No music played, no conversation was had. The Bad Boy drove in silence, and Valeria fidgeted repeatedly.

It was the most awkward car journey Valeria had ever experienced. After all the years of great memories shared in this car, she felt as if they were destroying them all. For what? A night of sex?

And what a night of sex it had been, lacking both chemistry, and well, sex.

Fabulous.

"I'll put these away and say goodbye to them for another year," the Bad Boy suddenly told Valeria, snapping her out of an avalanche of negative thoughts. She watched him as he opened the compartment in front of her as he drove, and threw the nearly full packet of condoms inside, slamming it shut.

Valeria forced a nervous laugh. "Yeah right, I'm sure you have another three chicks lined up this week alone," she told him with a slight smile, and he turned to look her in the eye as he drove.

"No I don't. I hardly have sex. I have a kid to look after."

Valeria gulped.

I mean, he's clearly still lying through his teeth, but he sure is going to a lot of trouble to make me feel special after the night of terror caused by, well, me.

"You don't have to take me back to the train station if Lily's town is before the station. You can drop me there and I'll make my way."

Valeria didn't mean it in a bitchy way, she simply didn't want to cause him any more trouble than she had already done or make him put any more effort than he had already done.

He glanced at her as if it was the most shocking suggestion he had ever heard Valeria make. "Val, I'm going to take you to the train station."

His gaze was so commanding and so authoritative, as if she didn't have a say in the matter, and so the only thing she could think to do was nod. They both took a deep and very awkward breath in, and exhaled at the same time.

He suddenly put on the radio, and a cheesy pop song played. Valeria didn't dare change the station, even though she really wanted to. Even though she hated the song playing.

She knew she could no longer change the radio station, she could no longer be the cute girl fighting for his attention in his black Audi. Those privileges had now disappeared, the second she had lured him to his uncle's cabin in the middle of nowhere for sex and then...didn't want sex.

It's not that I don't have the right to say no, of course I do. It's just that saying no has now come with a price, given our entire friendship was based on an incredible sexual tension that no longer exists.

She couldn't giggle flirtatiously, she couldn't poke him in the chest like she used to, and she couldn't sing along to the crappy songs at the top of her lungs to make him laugh. She had lost all those rights when she had agreed to go with him to his uncle's cabin. Or perhaps she had lost those rights when she had said no to sex.

Was it the promise of sex that had ruined us or the lack thereof?

Valeria wasn't sure. She just knew that twelve hours earlier she had had a friend, and now she didn't. That their beautiful and unique rapport was lost forever, and that this realisation made her very sad.

As Valeria thought about all these things, they suddenly entered a small town completely covered in snow, and she gasped.

"Yep. This town always get hit," he told her, and she thought about how even talking about snow made them awkward.

She decided not to speak at all, that it was easier this way, and so instead of responding, instead of expressing her love for snow or sharing memories from childhood spent in the snow, she decided to keep quiet. To sink into the awkwardness, to not disturb it, to close her eyes and hope that it eventually went away.

She couldn't sleep though. She couldn't escape the awkwardness. It was so intense that she could hardly look at him, let alone confront the situation. It was like she was being punished for going out to the cabin with the Bad Boy, or for not having sex with him.

Which one is it?

Valeria couldn't process properly in that car. She had to get out of there. She had to think. She had to understand what had happened.

It was an entire hour later that they arrived at the train station, and Valeria instantly unclicked her seatbelt. "Thank you."

"Wait, I'll come with you, check the train times-"

"No, don't worry! I'll check all of that."

He stared at her with confusion. "Val, I'll come with you-"

"No, I'm fine don't worry," Valeria interrupted him, and she knew her 'no' had come too quick.

"It's not a problem, Valeria. Let me come with you."

But Valeria didn't want him with her. She wanted to get away from him, from this situation. She needed to, as soon as possible.

"I'm a big girl," she told him, reassuringly.

To Valeria's relief, he nodded, and loosened his hand on his seatbelt. The awkwardness between them hit maximum level.

"Alright, well, this was fun, erm, it was...good...."

He suddenly clutched his seatbelt again. "Come on Val, let me take you into the train station-"

"No, no, no! I'll find the next train myself, don't you worry."

Please get me out of this awkward car!

Yet when Valeria looked at the Bad Boy she saw disappointment and helplessness. No matter what they had gone through together over the years, the Bad Boy had always been there to help her. To make sure she was okay.

Something inside of her felt terrible, and she knew she had to do damage control. She looked over at the window in the train station and squinted. "Look, I think I see the train times from here, next one is in fourteen minutes...I think?! I'd better hurry and get my ticket, if I want to go and surprise Pattie!"

The Bad Boy hesitated before replying. "Right."

Valeria debated giving him a hug but voted against it, having flashbacks of the previous night come rushing back to her as she remembered their naked bodies touching. When they were never supposed to. When that line was never supposed to be crossed.

"See you soon, Val. Text me if you have any problems with the train, I'll come and pick you up."

"Sure, thanks. I'm sure I'll be fine."

Valeria stumbled out of the car with her luggage, and raced into the train station without ever looking back.

It was the fastest Valeria had ever run with luggage in hand, and she didn't stop until she got to the ticket office.

She sighed as she looked up at the screen: The next train to the small town would depart in three hours and forty-five minutes.

41

Valeria stood outside the bar, *their* bar, with nothing but memories flooding her mind. Moments she and the Bad Boy had shared together after nine whole years.

Except this time, she couldn't remember the feelings that had made her crazy about him. In fact, her memories felt as if they had happened to someone else, and she had just somehow stored them in her mind.

The night away at the cabin had only happened forty-eight hours ago, yet it felt like an entire century had passed. Valeria had text the Bad Boy to tell him she had arrived home, he had replied 'okay good to hear' and that had been it. They had not spoken since.

Valeria looked up at the bar, reliving ghosts of herself from the past nine years – all the hairdos, the fashion choices, the things that had been said. The summer nights that had been lived and that would never return.

She saw herself at sixteen, drunk with the Bad Boy and his secret girlfriend, Lena. She hardly remembered anything about her as a person, but she remembered her face – the big brown eyes, the beautiful smooth skin. The Bad Boy had always had impeccable taste in women.

She saw herself at eighteen, being chased around the benches by the Bad Boy with ice cream that eventually spilled onto his leather jacket and had her in shrieks of laughter.

She was able to envision the countless times they had left the bar at last call, completely and utterly wasted.

Their first kiss.

Every time they had ever touched.

His smile.

It all seemed to mean nothing to Valeria now, and it frustrated her. It made her feel as if her heart had tricked her all this time, for all these years. She felt as if when she visited the small town, nothing ever seemed to make any sense.

"You ready?!" Pattie wailed, snapping Valeria out of her memories. She turned around to see Pattie skipping across the street over to her. Dressed in a huge winter coat with the hood up, Valeria laughed at Pattie's excited face popping out from the coat.

"You look like an eskimo!"

"Good, eskimo are cute!" Pattie told her, throwing an arm around her as she shivered loudly. "It's about bloody time me and you have a proper night out, it's been too long."

The ladies both looked up at the bar, and Pattie rubbed Valeria's shoulder. "Shall we go inside?"

Valeria was hesitant to do so without the Bad Boy; she didn't want to trample on their memories. Yet she also knew that due to the continuous snowstorm they were currently finding themselves in that this was the only option; the other bars were way too far from the small town.

"Yep," she replied, and so they marched into the bar. The hot air hit their faces instantly and they smiled at one another as they unwrapped themselves. The only free table was one in the corner; the same table that the Bad Boy and herself usually sat at.

You're fine. So what if you came here a few times with the Bad Boy? It doesn't mean it's your bar, Val.

You're here with Pattie now. You can make new memories. Better memories. Different memories. You can do it!

Though Valeria believed the words she told herself, it only took three seconds for her mind to be invaded by an avalanche of memories. And this time, she remembered the feelings too.

She remembered the way the Bad Boy had sat opposite her with that smile of his; that warmth in his eyes that he always thought she couldn't see.

She remembered his laugh, and how it gave her this warm feeling in her stomach.

She remembered the first time she tried an Irish coffee with him; she remembered how good and safe she had always felt with him at 3am.

She remembered how good she felt in his company, how they could talk for hours.

She remembered that game they used to play where you'd have to guess what the relationship between the strangers around you were.

She remembered looking out the window at the darkness of the small town and talking about life and what they wanted to achieve. The important, personal, intimate stuff seemed to always roll off their tongues when they were together.

These memories continued to invade Valeria's mind, to remind her of their unique rapport, of how special the Bad Boy was to her. They were tearing her apart, and she suddenly missed him so much she needed to drink to temporarily block it all out.

Pattie joined her, without having a clue of the pain Valeria was currently going through. The flashbacks however didn't stop or even slow down with alcohol; they only accelerated.

Valeria and Pattie laughed a lot together though and had a good time. Valeria learned to ignore the flashbacks, but as she did so she couldn't help wondering what he was doing that night, and whether he was thinking about her too.

By the time Valeria headed home she was incredibly drunk, and her desire to text the Bad Boy began to surface. There was so much she wanted to say. So much she wanted the Bad Boy to know, before it was too late. Before too much time could pass. Their rapport was too special to be lost in such a careless manner.

Or maybe, it was just too special to lose at all. She whipped out her phone as she reached the porch of her house and, she began to type at warp speed...

42

Valeria

6:03AM: I don't know what happened the other night. But I've been thinking about it for two days straight. Maybe I was nervous, maybe we planned it too much. I also realised that we hadn't seen each other in a long time and that maybe just assuming we could run away to a cabin together without building rapport again was too ambitious of us, I don't know. I just want you know I'm really sorry and I don't want to lose you I
6:05AM: Sorry, my finger slipped and sent the text, I'm a bit drunk. But I mean every word of the above.
6:06AM: Good morning and I hope you have a good day.

The Bad Boy

7:03AM: Good morning! Wow you are the most incredibly accurate drunk texter I know.

Val are you crazy, don't apologise please, we are not robots. You're right, we can't plan things like that, it doesn't work. I hope I didn't make you feel uncomfortable in any way and I'm glad you were able to tell me no instead of go through something you didn't want. Of course you're not going to lose me, I'll always be here.

Valeria

11:45AM: Thanks, Leo. I'm glad to hear that.

The Bad Boy

11:47AM: Oh look who's up! Still drunk? Where did you go last night?

Valeria

11:51AM: Geoffrey's. But it was boring as fuck without you. What about you?

The Bad Boy

11:59AM. Ah nice, yeah things are always less fun without me around, I know.

12:00PM: I was with my daughter, I've had her for a couple of days now and let Lily deal with some family stuff. She'll go back tomorrow so I'm taking her sledging in the mountains this afternoon, she's very excited.

12:01PM: You leave the day after tomorrow, right?

Valeria

12:15PM: Ah that sounds lovely, I didn't realise you were still with her! Hope you're both having a good time together :)

12:16PM: Yep, I leave in 2 days.

The Bad Boy

12:19PM: Hey, you wanna come with us? I'll be taking my snowboard and I could teach you? I know you've always wanted to learn. I promise not to injure you haha

Valeria

12:28PM: Oh I would looooove to but I already promised Pattie I'd hang out with her this afternoon. Let's see each other before I leave though? Tomorrow night?

The Bad Boy

12:31PM: Yeah let's go for dinner. Have fun with Pattie!

Valeria

12:32PM: And you with Annabelle! I'm glad I've still got you. And you me, of course.

Bad Boy

12:36PM: Always, Val. Always.

43

It was 9pm and pouring down with rain when twenty-three-year old Valeria stepped outside Pattie's. She smiled and grabbed a newspaper from Pattie's coffee table before she jogged towards the black Audi parked at the edge of the driveway.

She remembered all the times this black Audi had arrived outside her house over the years. She remembered how much happiness and joy seeing this very car had brought her over the years. And now she knew that what had been happening here had not been a romance, but a blossoming friendship.

A really special friendship. A friendship worth saving. A friendship so strong it could survive one night of their futile attempts to across the borders of their friendship into sex. She knew that their friendship was strong enough to survive this.

Valeria jumped into the car, the Bad Boy turning to look at her, and suddenly the ghastly tension between them hit her smack in the face.

Wait, what?

I thought we were okay?!

Why are we still tense and awkward?!

They *hey'd* each other awkwardly, and the Bad Boy drove them off and away from the small town.

The journey quickly became unexpectedly difficult and uncomfortable. In fact, it was just as difficult and uncomfortable as when they had left each other at the train station just a few days earlier.

It was as if their texts the day before had not happened at all. As if no matter how much they had cleared things up via messages, the way they were face-to-face was only recording their last physical encounter.

Yet Valeria refused to sink into an awkward tension where it felt as if they were strangers, where it felt as if they were starting all over again.

She switched on the radio and a terribly poppy song blasted from the speakers. She looked over at the Bad Boy and he gave her a playfully annoyed look. Yet it didn't feel quite as natural as they had both had hoped. For one, the Bad Boy's playfully annoyed look was clearly forced.

Valeria wanted desperately to save their friendship, and she truly believed that there would be a way, yet she also knew that when she looked at him, she had flashbacks of his naked body on top of hers, and it made her mentally cringe.

Rejecting the reality of the situation, Valeria switched radio channel – again, and again, and again, and again. Yet his playfully annoyed face remained forced, and Valeria gulped, eventually giving up.

Perhaps forcing their friendship back on the scene wasn't the way to do this. They had always been natural with one another, it was where their chemistry came from, and so she decided to remain quiet.

She remained this way the entire remainder of the trip, staring out the window to keep flashbacks of their supposed sexual encounter at bay.

The journey felt like it lasted a lifetime, when in reality it was no longer than fifteen minutes.

When they arrived at the Chinese restaurant, it was empty, and they chose a table right in the middle of the venue.

As they sat down, Valeria realised that over all the years they had known each other, they had never gone out for dinner together, not even once. And that there was something nice about doing it now, something natural. Something that seemed to dispel all the tension between them in the car.

Well, nearly all of it.

"What would you like to drink?" the Bad Boy asked her, and as Valeria looked at him sitting opposite her with a menu in hand, she couldn't help but smile. She would never in a million years have guessed that this was the Bad Boy's favourite restaurant.

"You choose for me," Valeria found herself saying, as if her trust in him had somehow returned. And as if he noticed the return of something too, he smiled sincerely at her before murmuring 'okay'.

"So how was it with Annabelle yesterday?" she asked him, as he eyed the menu.

"Oh, brilliant. She loves going sledging."

"Nice!"

"Yeah, and then I sat her down for her Sunday history lesson."

Valeria frowned. "Her *what?*"

"Every Sunday I give her a history lesson on the world. It's very important to me that she learns about how we got here, why the world is the way it is."

Valeria studied the Bad Boy, and they held a curious gaze across the table for a few moments. It occurred to Valeria that she had forgotten just how passionate about politics and history and equal rights the Bad Boy really was. She had also forgotten just how much she admired this about him.

"What are you teaching her about at the moment?"

"Everything. The politics of our country, of the rest of the Europe-"

"You mean your conspiracy theories!" Valeria shrieked, with a grin.

"Excuse me, they're not conspiracy theories. I've told you these before, there's proof that-"

"Yeah, yeah! Sure, Leo. Please tell me again, how is it that you think these conspiracy theories can possibly be true..."

As the waiter waited patiently for his only customers to be ready to order, the pair began playfully arguing about the Bad Boy's so-called conspiracy theories.

And just like that, the true nature of the friendship between the Bad Boy and Valeria returned, and the waiter realised, rather annoyingly, that they weren't going to be done anytime soon.

44

"What?" the Bad Boy suddenly asked her across the table at the Chinese restaurant, and Valeria realised she had been continuously staring at him and smiling for the best part of the last fifteen minutes.

"No, nothing, I just think you're full of BS," she told him, just as their food arrived.

They were still the only customers in the restaurant and therefore had the undivided attention of the only waiter on the floor.

"Can I get you anything else?" he asked them, as he placed the plates down in front of them.

"Uh, actually, yes, do you have any fortune cookies?" the Bad Boy asked him, and Valeria frowned. The waiter disappeared to fetch a couple and she gave the Bad Boy a puzzled look.

"Fortune cookies are the best thing about this place and I'd rather we open them now than at the end of the meal. They're, uh, a little unconventional," the Bad Boy told her. "Anyway, why exactly am I full of BS? I'm going to send you the titles of some books for when you're back in the city."

Both of their faces seemed to darken as soon as the words 'back in the city' were uttered.

Valeria was due to go back in twenty-four hours and she didn't want to leave. She was quickly remembering why she had been friends with the Bad Boy for nine years, but even more importantly, why she had liked him.

Why she still liked him.

Yes, her feelings of lust for the Bad Boy were back. They came back in waves as soon as they sat down at the Chinese restaurant and were only getting stronger, and tenser, the more time that went by. The more they spoke, and bonded, and laughed together again, the more she craved him.

She wanted to touch him, to be close to him, to hear him laugh. She didn't understand what was going on, and she was well aware that just a few days earlier she had had him to herself in a cabin in the middle of nowhere and had not wanted to have sex with him.

Yet that feeling was no longer around. It was now replaced with lust and chemistry and passion, and she knew she was finally ready.

The Bad Boy, as if also picking up on the sexual vibes that were back on the table, was smiling and joking more than normal. In fact, with the amount of times he smiled during that dinner he hardly looked like a Bad Boy at all.

"So have you made a decision yet?" the Bad Boy asked her, halfway through their meal. He was referring to the big life decision that Valeria had to make when she got back to the city. She currently worked as a designer at an advertising agency and had been offered the chance to join a worldwide famous brand. Though she loved her job, she wasn't sure she could reject such a huge opportunity for her career.

"I think you should take it," the Bad Boy added. "I can see you at a big brand. You deserve it, Val. You're going to do big things. A big role like that? It will suit you."

Valeria loved how well the Bad Boy knew her, and just how much he believed in her. It just never seemed to go away, no matter what they went through together.

The pair stared at one another with intrigue, with lust, with hunger, but also with an immense of care for one another.

Their moment was however interrupted by the waiter returning with two fortune cookies.

"You first," the Bad Boy said with a smile, as the waiter stood in front of them, clearly bored at work and dying to see what their fortune cookies would say.

They both watched Valeria as she nervously opened her fortune cookie and pulled out the piece of paper.

You already know what you want.

She smiled, and showed the two eager pair of eyes looking back at her.

"There you go! You know it already. You just need to make your move."

And though the Bad Boy was talking about her career, Valeria knew she had something completely different in mind.

45

The Bad Boy parked up in front of Valeria's house, yet Valeria didn't notice as she was continuously poking the Bad Boy in the chest. She had been doing this for the most part of the journey home, and the pair of them had enjoyed every touch they shared. There was more sexual chemistry between them in that one evening than in their nine-year friendship. Valeria was excited.

She was incredibly hungry for the Bad Boy now; she envisioned the eight different positions she wanted to have sex with him in, she envisioned the kisses, the touches, the orgasms. There was no doubt about it this time; she wanted him, and she wanted him *bad*.

What a fool she had been to give up sex with him, what a fool she had been to have not taken advantage of having an entire weekend with the body in front of her.

Valeria didn't know what had happened out in the cabin, but she reckoned it was the whole scheduling sex fiasco that had caused her body to tense, and her libido to run a mile.

But now, now things were different. Things were definitely heating up again, and it was time to explode. To explore each other's bodies. To *finally* and *truly* give into their wild desires for one another.

After nine whole years, it was about time.

"Have you had enough yet?!" the Bad Boy told her with a grin, acting playfully annoyed. "We're here, you know."

Valeria continued to poke the Bad Boy, ignoring his words. He suddenly grabbed both her hands with one hand, and poked her in the chest. She squealed, yet she could feel her libido waking up, standing up and taking notice.

"You like that? Yeah? You like that?" he continued to poke her and she continued to squeal. His face drew nearer and nearer and to hers, and as she squealed and giggled like a fourteen-year-old girl, they found each other's faces sitting centimetres apart.

Suddenly Valeria stopped laughing. She looked intensely into the Bad Boy's eyes, and he looked back in curiosity. His eyes dotted back and forth from her eyes to her lips, from her eyes to her lips.

Valeria was ready to move forward, to attack him with a full-on kiss, but he coughed awkwardly and turned to the window before she could have a chance. He nodded at the torrential rain outside.

"Maybe we should wait a few minutes until it calms down. You'll get soaked."

Valeria's disappointment in missing her opportunity to kiss him was soon replaced by excitement at having a bit more time with him in the car. After all, this would be the last time she would see the Bad Boy in a while, possibly a year, and she wanted, more than anything in the world, to kiss him, and have sex with him, and show him that she wanted him.

He's not making a move because he thinks you don't want him. So you need to lead and show him that that is not the case.

Valeria knew there was only one thing for her to do. There was only one thing she *could* do.

She suddenly leapt across the clutch and attempted to kiss him. The Bad Boy however, jumped back in time and kept her back with his hands on her shoulders.

"Woah! No, no, Val, no, what are you doing?"

Valeria smiled, a little drunk from their Chinese beers. "I'm ready now, Leo, I feel it. I feel our chemistry." She attempted to kiss him again but he again held her back by the shoulders.

"No, Val, I thought our dinner was about saving our friendship?"

"Yes, but I also realised I want you. I know you want me too. There's no need to be afraid, I want to try again, I am *sure...*" Valeria slid her hand over to the Bad Boy's trousers. "That things will be different this time."

Valeria took her hand away and moved back into her seat. The Bad Boy sighed in relief.

"Val, I think we've had too much to drink and..."

As the Bad Boy rambled on, Valeria couldn't help thinking: *Poor guy. After our shitty attempt at sex at his cabin he's terrified to try again.*

As he continued to ramble on, Valeria decided to take her top off. The Bad Boy stopped, mid-sentence, as she sat there in her red bra, beaming at him.

"Val, wait-"

"I'm ready now," she said so softly it was almost a whisper, and she leaned in to kiss him. Again however the Bad Boy stopped her at the shoulders, this time looking her directly in the eye with focus and sincerity.

"Valeria, listen to me. I don't want to have sex with you."

2019

December

46

When Valeria returned to the small town, it felt as if she had been gone at least a year. In reality, it was only six weeks, but so much had happened in those six weeks that it felt like a much older version of herself.

Yet it was good to be back. It felt good. It felt right. This was her town as much as it was anyone's. She had every right to return, though I guess no one had expected it to be quite so soon.

Everyone she had bumped into in the small town so far had pointed out that she had last been there six weeks, as if she didn't already know. As if she could possibly forget her last exit from the small town.

Valeria walked around Pattie's infamous Christmas party in the beautiful red dress she had bought as a treat for herself when she had accepted her new job offer. She was now a senior designer for a major brand. She was making the big bucks.

As Valeria walked around the party, she felt contentment, and pride, and gratitude for the person she was, the person she had become. She had worked a long time to get to this point in life, and she was enjoying having arrived.

She watched Pattie laugh and joke with her brother, Max, across the huge room. It made her smile, and she was glad that at twenty-three years old she was finally able to make one of Pattie's Christmas parties. They were legendary in all circuits.

She re-lived the locals asking her why she was back so soon. "This place gives me clarity," she responded every time, and she stood by her answer. The small town had always cleared her head for her, and though she was happy and successful, she felt she needed to find some self-clarity. And maybe, the best way to get over certain things was to face them. Sometimes, when truly horrible things are said, their words, and their looks, can haunt you even when everything else is going so well in your life...

Valeria gawped at the Bad Boy, who looked at her as if she was seeing through her.

"What?" Valeria managed to say.

"I'm sorry, Valeria. I don't want to have sex with you." His words were sincere, she knew it, and this only further hurt her.

Stunned at the unexpected punch to the stomach, anger took over and Valeria threw her car door open.

"Fuck you, Leo." She yelled, and from that, she stormed out of the Bad Boy's car in her bra and marched into the torrential rain to her front door.

Valeria snapped back to reality and took a deep breath in. After all, she was over it. She had taught herself to be better than that, to let it be and move on in these six weeks.

She was intelligent, successful and beautiful both on the inside and out. She didn't need the Bad Boy to like her to be okay.

"Val," said a voice suddenly, and Valeria turned around to find Ben standing in front of her.

She frowned, surprised at just how much he had aged in only a few years. He had a few wrinkles now and his eyes seemed older too, though he was still just as handsome as the last time she had seen him.

Which was right before the Bad Boy and I accidentally a man who had assaulted me.

Fun times.

"Oh, hey Ben! How are you?"

Valeria had not spoken to Ben in years, given that the last time that they had seen each other, Ben had left Valeria drunk on the dance floor after she had drunkenly insulted him.

She was relaxed around him now as she knew he wasn't the most malevolent of people and that he likely didn't mean it to lead to trouble.

Still, you should probably not leave a vulnerable person alone when you know they have no other way to get home.

Since that night, Valeria saw Ben as a classic example of a coward. Yet over the years, her anger towards him seemed to die down and now she felt no strong feelings towards him, negative or not.

"I'm good, I'm a model and live in the city. Home for Christmas."

"Ah nice! Model suits you big time," she told him, referring to his good looks.

"Thanks, I think?! How about you? Heard from Pattie you're a big shot designer now, that's great to hear."

When did we all grow up? When did we stop being kids who spent their summers working shitty jobs to pay for our evening antics at the same bars with the gorgeous mountainous views?

When did I become...an adult?

"Listen," Ben continued, before Valeria could respond. "I wanted to apologise. I've been wanting to apologise for a long time. I shouldn't have left you that night. I know what happened next, and I'm really, truly sorry.

I think we (men) forget how much risk there is to getting home alone. I really, truly didn't think about those possibilities. I just thought you'd walk and it'd be fine. I would *never* purposely put a woman or girl's life in danger like that. I'm really, truly sorry."

Ben's voice sounded sincere and spoke straight to Valeria's heart.

"Thank you," she told him. "That really means a lot – your apology. I know you didn't mean any harm. However, as you said, we need to all be thinking more about the risks involved in those types of situations. And on my part, I'm really sorry for the horrible things I said that night. I was hurt by something else." Valeria paused. "Wait, how do you know about what happened…?"

Ben shook his head in anger and disappointment. "It's a small town, Val. Surrounded by other small towns. And all the older generations spend their days and nights looking out the window. You were seen from across the hill by the adjacent town."

As Valeria stared at Ben, she realised for the first time that people really are not straightforward. There's so many layers to every single human being on the planet. It's about knowing which cons you're not willing to put up with in the long term.

"So, we okay?" Ben asked.

Valeria smiled. "Have you had any of Pattie's sangria yet?" she asked him, as she put her arm around him and they walked across the semi-packed dance floor together.

The Bad Boy

Hey Val so I heard you're back in town. How long you here for? Fancy a drink tonight?

The Bad Boy

I'm back in town for a drink with Stevie, fancy catching up after?

The Bad Boy

You have to eventually stop ignoring me. Preferably before you leave.

47

Valeria stood at the bottom of the snowy hill, staring at her phone. It was eerily quiet around her without anyone in sight, and the air was so cold it could cut your skin if you were not careful.

She breathed out water vapour, as she continued to stare at her phone screen. Minutes went by, and around her it was starting to get dark. It was only 3pm, but it was already starting to get dark.

This is what she got when she visited the small town in winter.

The icy wind blew, but Valeria didn't move. Her eyes continued to remain fixated on the screen in front of her, or more, the draft message staring back at her.

Hey Leo, I'm not sure I'm going to have time. I head home in two days and I'm fully booked up till then. I'll be back soon though!

Ben suddenly sent her a text, telling her to hurry up and get to the party. Valeria took a deep breath in, and pressed 'send'.

It was gone, finally. Her decision had been made, finally. After an entire week's worth of indecisiveness, or ignoring all three of his messages, she was finally able to respond, to make a choice.

And she would stick to it, this time.

Satisfied with her decision, Valeria began to make her way up the snowy hill. It was really starting to get dark now, and scary, but she had to do it. She had a burning desire inside of her to climb this hill, to reach to the top.

She began breathing heavily as she did so, her legs starting to ache too, but she kept going. She kept fighting against the icy cold wind, against the aching legs, against her frustratingly out of shape self, because she needed to get to the top, to achieve her goal, to *see* that she could do it.

By the time she made it to the top of the snowy hill, it was pitch black. Exhaling deeply (and loudly) she looked around at all the blinking lights beneath her. She was finally calm, finally pleased with herself. For she had achieved what she wanted.

She smiled as her breathing began to slow, and took it all in, proudly.

She didn't know why, but as Valeria looked out at the clusters of small towns, she began to experience flashbacks from every single trip she had ever taken to the small town. Every barbecue, every bike ride, every happy moment she had ever experienced there.

It's strange how life works, Valeria thought to herself. *It's those moments that don't seem special at all in the moment that mostly turn out to be your favourite moments when you look back.*

When you see, in retrospect, that they were the most important moments of all.

Valeria envisioned herself at Pattie's when the Bad Boy had walked in to pick her up for their first ever night out. She had been sixteen, naïve and desperate for adventure.

She remembered the look on the Bad Boy's young seventeen-year-old face when he had walked into the kitchen, the way he had looked at Valeria as if, yes, finally, you are mine for the evening.

Valeria had flashbacks of her summer with Ben, the countless times they had got drunk together. Parties thrown with Pattie. Every single bike ride she had ever experienced and enjoyed in the small town.

She knew then this was her town. That it had always been her town. That it would always be her town. For it was in this very town, that most of Valeria's growing up had taken place.

It was a part of her. It was a part she would never be able to let go of, even if she ever wanted to.

Valeria stayed at the top of that snowy hill for a good ten minutes, despite the freezing cold, despite the need to get to the party as soon as possible. She needed this, and she knew she was letting go of what she needed to let go. Something was leaving her, something big, and she eventually felt better. She smiled to herself, as she waved goodbye to a weight she had kept hold of for too long.

And before she knew it, it was gone. And all that remained was the good.

Descending from atop the snowy hill, Valeria couldn't help smiling to herself in relief. In a satisfaction she had never felt before.

In order to get to Ben's, Valeria needed to walk. A snowstorm had hit the small town and the adjacent towns a few days earlier, and since then, all residents had been snowed in.

Trains and buses were not currently running, and Valeria was aware that she could not get back to the city until the snowstorm blew over.

She made her way back down the hill successfully, and knew that now came the tricky part; walking on the ice.

The entire way to Ben's was on an icy pathway across the main road. There was no footpath, just road, and the roads were empty due to the ice. Yet, if Valeria wanted to make it to his party, to celebrate the New Year with Ben and his friends, she knew this was the only way.

Feeling particularly courageous as of late, Valeria slowly began to walk across the ice in her knee-high winter boots. She walked slowly, knowing it was a mile-long walk to Ben's and it was already dark, yet it didn't stop her.

No cars passed and white surrounded Valeria as she walked. She feared for her safety, she feared she would drop down to her death just as the trucker all those years ago. She feared someone just like the trucker would appear and repeat history, just with a different ending.

An ending that could ruin her life. An ending where Valeria couldn't save herself.

Yet she was able to fight against the fear, to accept it existed within her, to be okay with it. Because fear was a normal part of life, and as long as she was careful with the things that scared her, she would always be fine.

Valeria carefully tread on the ice with each step, fearing each one would be her last. And as she did so, the silence that encompassed her was slowly interrupted as she slowly heard the sound of a helicopter.

Though Valeria had never seen or heard a helicopter upclose, she was sure that it was one. And it didn't half surprise her, given there was no other transportation available. In states of emergency, she imagined that helicopters were used.

She listened curiously as she continued to walk, and walk, against the icy cold winter, against the ice beneath her that was just waiting to make her slip. Valeria tried to guess where the helicopter was landing – the sounds were getting closer and closer, and yet, she could deduct that the sound was not coming from Ben's town.

By the time Valeria got to his house she was exhausted, more physically than mentally – it took a lot to tell yourself over and over to tread carefully. Especially if you were a fast walker.

She knocked on Ben's big red wooden door, and it flung open. Pop music blasted, heat hit her face, and Ben stood in front of her carrying a bottle of Valeria's favourite wine. People could be heard talking in the background – it seemed like quite a big gathering.

"Well it's about bloody time!" Ben said. "Ready to start the New Year in style?!"

They hugged and Valeria rushed to get herself away from the cold and into the warmth. She closed the door behind her, knowing that she had made it. That she was safe, just like she had been so determined to be the whole walk over.

See, a piece of cake.

There was a sudden scream, and everyone rushed into the living room to see Tamara, a girl Valeria had spoken to a few times over the years, hanging up her phone with trembling hands.

"There's been a motorbike accident just outside of town." Tamara's eyes narrowed to Valeria, and Valeria knew what was coming before the words were even uttered.

"It's Leo... He and his motorbike were badly hit by a lorry at the corner of Finn Street."

48

Valeria had never run so fast in her entire life. She had never wanted to get somewhere so fast and so badly in all twenty-three years of her existence.

Luckily there was a shortcut to the way to the corner of Finn Street and it was through the snow and not the ice.

Valeria bolted out of Ben's house as soon as she heard that Leo had been an accident. She still had Ben's champagne bottle in her hand and she threw it into the snow as she ran. Nothing else in the entire world mattered in that moment.

Just the Bad Boy's safety.

Just the Bad Boy's health.

Just to see and make sure the Bad Boy was okay.

That the Bad Boy was going to be okay.

"He's such a rebel, thinks he's James Dean," Valeria recalled his mum, Barbara, saying when she was fourteen.

"I'm not afraid of danger. Racing gives me something nothing else can, and if it kills me, so be it. It would be worth it," Valeria recalled the Bad Boy's words to her one night at their bar when she was eighteen or nineteen.

She was terrified for the Bad Boy's life, knowing that he was without limits. Knowing that he was one to race on his motorbike, even in a snowstorm. This stuff didn't phase him, and sometimes, Valeria felt as if he took pleasure from tempting danger like that.

And she knew very well that that sort of approach to life could sometimes lead to fatality.

She tried to accelerate as much as her legs could take, desperate to see him, to help him.

She could finally see the corner up ahead, the corner that Tamara had mentioned. It was a corner that the Bad Boy had raced past with her at the back many times. She had always thought it was a huge blind spot, but she had never said anything as she hadn't wanted to seem like a coward.

She had, after all, wanted to seem invincible, just like the Bad Boy.

Valeria raced and raced until she got to the corner of Finn Street and turned, gasping at the sight in front of her. There the Bad Boy lay, spread out in the middle of the road, blood everywhere.

He was awake and yelling in terrible pain. Valeria fought back tears and sadness at the sound of his pain, of what could be happening to him. She had to hide her fear, her worry, for the Bad Boy.

"Leo!" she yelled desperately. The road was closed off, the helicopter parked nearby as four paramedics tended to him. Valeria hopped over the barriers, continuing to call his name. She dropped down to the floor next to him, and she could now properly see him.

The blood.

The pain in his eyes.

The fear.

The paramedics analysing every inch of his body.

"Leo," Valeria began, "Leo."

The Bad Boy's eyes seemed to brighten slightly. "Val? Val?"

"I'm here, I'm here," and she instinctively took his hand and squeezed it. "You're going to be okay."

"Val? Val, I'm so glad you're here-"

Valeria had to keep taking deep breaths in to hold back the tears, the pain, the sadness. She ached for his pain, as if the pain was being experienced just as intensely by Valeria as it was by the Bad Boy.

"Everything is going to be okay, Leo. Relax, take deep breaths in, these lovely paramedics are going to fly you out to the best hospital, you're going to be okay-"

"Val, I'm scared. I'm scared."

"I'm right here Leo, everything is going to be fine."

As the paramedics put Leo on a stretch bed, one of them turned to Valeria. "Are you coming with us?"

49

Valeria had never been on a helicopter before. In-between the shock and worry for the Bad Boy's life, she found her trembling hands could not work out how to put on her seatbelt. One of the paramedics helped her, smiling slightly at her before going back to tending to the Bad Boy.

There were now tubes coming out of his nose and arms, and he was becoming paler by the second. Valeria held his hand, tightly, as the paramedics continued to tend to him.

The pain that Valeria felt as she held his hand, as she watched him suffer, as she wondered whether he would survive, was something Valeria had never felt before. She had been blessed with having all her loved ones still being alive so far in life, but she was sure that what she felt, the pain that transpired within her in that moment, was some sort of love.

She had always cared, always loved the Bad Boy. *No matter what.*

No matter what he did. No matter how many times he hurt her. No matter how many shitty things he said to her. She knew, deep down, that though the Bad Boy was a complex person, he cared about her. He wanted the best for her, just as she did for him.

And this, this right here, was all that mattered.

Not whether they were both sexually attracted to one another. Not if they could have a successful romantic relationship together.

None of this mattered. What they had, what they shared, was an incredibly rapport, and life was not as black and white as being *either* platonic *or* romantic.

Society told you that these are the boundaries, but it's not true. There's so many more layers to the rapport between two people, just as there are many layers to a person.

When Valeria realised this, she learnt to let go of her nine-year desire to define her relationship with the Bad Boy. She no longer cared whether they were friends or something more. On the bigger scale of life, it did not matter.

All that mattered was that she cared for the man lying on the bed in front of her, and all that mattered was the man lying in the bed in front of her healed as quick as humanly possible.

"Everything is going to be okay," she whispered, and she wondered where this strength came from. She wanted to crumble, to burst into tears, but she couldn't. She *knew* she had to remain strong for the Bad Boy.

Once they landed on the roof of the hospital, Valeria could only stand back and watch as the paramedics carried the bed with the Bad Boy on it off the helicopter and into the hospital.

"Excuse me, where are you taking him?" Valeria asked, still managing to remain strong.

"He's going straight into surgery," replied the same paramedic that had put on her seatbelt for her. She watched them disappear into the hospital, and it took a few moments, but the breakdown that Valeria had anticipated arrived.

It hit her harder than she could have ever imagined and she burst into hysterical tears in only a matter of seconds.

Okay, Valeria.

Take a deep breath in...

50

Never had Valeria felt more embarrassed, more ashamed of herself. There was silence between them and all that could be heard was the rain pitter-pattering on the car windows.

The Bad Boy didn't say anything either, he just looked at her for a reaction as she took in the words 'I don't want to have sex with you, Valeria.'

She gulped, unable to remain in this car, with the person in front of her.

"Fuck you, Leo," she hissed at him with venom, before aggressively clicking her car door open and bursting out into the torrential rain.

"Val!" he called after her, but she marched through the rain with only one goal on her mind: To get as far away from the person now chasing her. She heard his car door click open and footsteps getting closer.

"Val!" he clutched her elbow but she violently shrugged him off.

"Get away from me Leo, get away from me! Stay the hell away from me. All you do is cause pain. I want more nothing to do with you.

In fact, if we never speak again, I'll die happy."

51

When Valeria walked into the hospital room, she had braced herself beforehand. She had told herself to be prepared. She had told herself that she needed to hold back all her sadness, because she needed to be strong.

For him.

When Valeria walked into the hospital room, she saw the Bad Boy lying in bed with tubes coming out of him. His eyes were closed, and, afraid to disturb him, she tiptoed across the room to his side. There was a chair, just one, untouched.

Nobody had come to visit him. Not even his ex-girlfriend Lily, the mother of his child. She was currently was out of the country and returning the following day.

Yet something felt weird, as if this in itself was a message, that being a Bad Boy didn't pay off, in the end. Keeping everyone at bay doesn't work out, in the end.

For anyone.

354

The Bad Boy suddenly shifted and opened his eyes, looking around the room before noticing Valeria by his side, smiling shyly at him.

"Hi," she whispered, as if talking at a normal decibel could harm him in some way.

"Hey," he managed, with the most affection she had never heard him use in his tone.

"How are you feeling?" Valeria asked him. She was glad that she was there, that she was able to help him. However, it felt strange to be his only visitor. He and his mother, Barbara, had had a fight the previous year and were not currently talking. His dad had always been a deadbeat dad who never provided for his family or demonstrated any love or affection towards his children (except for that one time he came to support him at the volleyball tournament when he was fifteen ironically). And his friends, well, he didn't have any, and his sister, Emily, was at some beach in the south of France, sending her regards.

The Bad Boy was, essentially, alone. Except for Valeria. He always had Valeria. He had always had Valeria.

"I've been better," he joked, trying to laugh but moaning in pain as his chest ached.

Valeria immediately got up. "Are you okay? Do you need me to get a doctor?" she asked, before turning to look at the door. "Excuse me!" she yelled to the door, torn between temporarily leaving him to fetch someone and staying by the Bad Boy's side to not allow him to be or feel alone.

"Val, I'm okay," the Bad Boy managed to say, "please, sit down."

She obeyed. She didn't question it nor challenge him like she usually did.

"You gave us quite the scare," she began, "but the doctors say, miracously, you're going to be alright, eventually. It will take a lot of physiotherapy, and your stitches however will be permanent and-"

"I said no because it felt like I was forcing you." The Bad Boy suddenly blurted out. Valeria opened her mouth to reply, to ask what he was talking about, when he continued. "When you wanted to have sex that night. Outside your house. It felt like you were forcing yourself because you felt you had to, like you owed me in some way, and I didn't want that. I didn't want you to feel like you had to. I didn't want it that way.

I know that was your choice to make, but I also know you value our relationship. That you wouldn't want to see it disappear, just as much as I don't.

I've always liked you, Val. I've always found you incredible. I've always loved being around you, even at a distance at fourteen. That genuine smile of yours, the way you care. The way you like to annoy me. Your touch. Your smell. Your everything.

I wanted to be around you and get to know you even when I was fifteen. Even before I knew anything about you. When my mum said you were asking about me, I asked her to tell me everything she knew about *you*, and I waited two long years for you to return. To accidentally show up when you would. It was no accident. I planned, and became friends with Pattie so that I could learn more about you. So that I could meet you, and be around you.

That night, when you asked to hang out and I was with Lena, it was me and Lena's six month anniversary, I was all ready to go and pick her up, and derailed the entire thing because I wanted to see you, to know you. And I knew back then, before knowing you, that you were going to be a hell of a lot more interesting than Lena, than the other girls since then.

When it was your eighteenth birthday and I went out to a party in another city, all I kept thinking about was you and how this was a once in a life time moment and I wanted to be there with you for it.

When we kissed on that mountain, every bone in my body yelled, *'tell her! Tell her the truth! Tell her Lily is pregnant!'*

When we got to that cabin and we were alone, it didn't feel right to me either, it felt forced, but I wanted *you* to have a good time. That is the only thing I care about."

But Val," the Bad Boy smiled, giving her a dopey smile as Valeria's eyes filled with tears. "Who else in the world would I ever steal croissants for?"

2020

52

As Valeria stood at the top of the snowy mountain, she looked around her at the gorgeous view. The view that still managed to take her breath away.

The mountains that would always inspire her, that would always be a part of her. She knew and recognised the power of the small town and its surroundings in a way that previous years had failed to do so. She was now a fully fledged adult, and she knew the full extent of the magic of what currently surrounded her.

The way it connected to her, and spoke to her, and stayed with her, no matter what.

She took a deep breath of fresh air in, and took in the silence of the beauty that surrounded her.

"*Hey!* Are you coming down or what?!" a voice snapped Valeria out of her thoughts and she looked down the snowy mountain to see the Bad Boy and his daughter, Isabel, in their matching blue jumpsuits, waving at her with grins on their faces.

Their happy eyes beamed back at her, waiting for her to join them.

Isabel sat on a sledge, impatiently waiting for Valeria with the Bad Boy's fatherly clutches on the sledge behind her.

"We haven't got all day!" the Bad Boy added.

"Yeah, hurry up, auntie Valeria!" Isabel yelled.

"Okay, okay!" Valeria shouted, as she balanced on her snowboard. "Keep your panties on," she muttered to herself. She took a deep breath in, and tilted forward, as she began to snowboard down the empty mountain.

The Bad Boy and Isabel *woo*'d and yelled encouraging things as Valeria clumsily yet successfully snowboarded down the mountain, even managing a couple of small jumps as she did so.

The feeling of freedom that encompassed was ecstasy. She was finally doing it, finally snowboarding alone, finally conquering the sport she had dreamed of conquering for the best part of the decade. And she had never felt more alive.

She wanted more than anything to look up, to see their proud looks, but she was terrified to lose her balance. Yet even if she didn't look, she could feel the Bad Boy's proud look. The look he had always had when she succeeded at anything. That look of, *I knew you could do it.*

I always knew.

Just as she got closer to the bottom of the mountain and their yells got louder and louder, Valeria suddenly lost focus and toppled over, landing on the snow on her butt.

She squealed unexpectedly (up until then she had been the cool snowboarder and she was disappointed to end with such a stereotypical girly squeal).

"*Woo!* Well done, auntie Val!" Isabel yelled, clapped her gloves together.

Quick footsteps drew closer and Valeria knew it was the Bad Boy before she saw him towering over her. He was grinning and he offered his hand. She took it and he lugged her up to her feet in a nanosecond. Sometimes Valeria forgot just how strong the Bad Boy really was.

"That was actually not bad," he told her, "I mean, after an entire winter's worth of lessons from yours truly, what do you expect?"

"*Daaad,* can we go back up now?" Isabel nagged him. "Auntie Valeria, sledge with me."

The Bad Boy walked over to his daughter. "Auntie Valeria sucks at sledging, you're better off with daddy, Is."

Valeria immediately scooped up some snow off the ground next to her, shaped it into a snowball, and through it at the Bad Boy's head.

Annabelle was in instant giggles, as the Bad Boy stopped, and waited a few seconds before he turned around. Valeria stood there with a big smile on her face.

"I think you'll find I'm actually much better at sledging than yourself, which is why Isabel prefers me as her designated driver. You do rather suck at all types of driving that exist in this world."

The Bad Boy's eyes lit up with playful rage and he took off, chasing her around the knee-high snow as she squealed and laughed, Isabel giggling loudly in the background.

"Get him, auntie Valeria! Get him!"

And like every time they had ever been in each other's presence, their touch was electric, a chemistry so rare, and unique, and inspiring, that they couldn't help but smile every time they shared it.

Read *Adriano Exists* from the same author!

Alexis Brunetti has done every music internship out there. Yet despite her efforts, nobody is hiring. Or at least, nobody is hiring *her*...

That is, until she accidentally crosses paths with multi-platinum award winning Italian singer, Paolo Petrinelli, and his band of colourful characters.

Lisa Sa grew up in north west London, and has been writing stories since she was seven years old. She first became a published author in 2017 with her debut book, *Canned Tuna,* and has since gone on to publish her first novel, *Adriano Exists,* in 2019.

She currently works as a strategist for a reputable marketing agency in London, where she does what she loves most – be a storyteller.

www.lisasawriting.com
www.instagram.com/lisasaauthor